TROUBLE IN LOVE

As soon as they arrived on the Cross County grounds, Stevie ran from the car. Lisa and Carole followed more slowly, heading for the horse van Max had brought from Pine Hollow. They could see Phil detach himself from a group of Cross County riders and hurry toward Stevie with a big smile on his face.

"Uh-oh," Lisa said. "Is that an invitation in Phil's hand?"

Carole looked and nodded. "Trouble," she said.

A moment later they could hear Stevie's shriek carried back to them on the wind: "What do you *mean* you don't want to go to my dance?"

THE SADDLE CLUB

STABLE HEARTS

BONNIE BRYANT

A SKYLARK BOOK
NEW YORK · TORONTO · LONDON · SYDNEY · AUCKLAND

RL 5, 009–012

STABLE HEARTS

A Bantam Skylark Book / February 1997

ISBN 0-553-48418-4

Published simultaneously in the United States and Canada.

PRINTED IN THE UNITED STATES OF AMERICA

OPM   0 9 8 7 6 5 4 3 2

I would like to express my special thanks to Kimberly Brubaker Bradley for her help in the writing of this book.

"PINK BREECHES! NOW I've seen everything!" Stevie Lake said, dropping the currycomb she was holding. Stevie's horse, Belle, was standing on crossties in the aisle of Pine Hollow Stables while Stevie groomed her. Belle swung her head around as if interested, and Stevie gave her a pat.

"Where?" asked Lisa Atwood, one of Stevie's two best friends. She looked up and down the aisle but didn't see anyone wearing breeches, besides herself. Lisa's were classic-cut beige ones, however.

"Pink? You're *not* serious!" Stevie's other best friend, Carole Hanson, sounded appalled. Carole was a very good and very correct rider. She knew that only traditional neutral colors, like beige, light gray, and rust, were considered suitable for the horse show ring. "I've never even heard of pink breeches," she declared.

Stevie laughed. "Have you heard of Veronica diAngelo?" she asked. She pointed out the window of Belle's nearby stall, and the three girls hurried into the stall for a closer look. Outside, in the stable's drive, Veronica, another Pine Hollow rider, had just gotten out of her family's chauffeur-driven Mercedes. She was wearing a white fluffy sweater and hot pink breeches. In the drab winter landscape, the breeches stuck out like a neon sign.

"*That's* pink," Lisa agreed. "I think my mom grows peonies that color."

Carole shut her eyes as if in great pain. "They don't make breeches that color," she said. "They can't. They *wouldn't*."

"I hope they do," Stevie said. "I'll get some. I think they're fantastic."

Carole groaned and Lisa giggled. Of the three of them, Stevie was by far the most flamboyant. She usually rode in tattered jeans and boots, because breeches were so tame.

"It could be a Saddle Club uniform," Lisa sug-

2

gested teasingly. "We could get matching pairs, and I could embroider a Saddle Club logo on the hip pockets."

Long ago the three friends had formed a club, The Saddle Club, dedicated to horses and each other. The only rules were that members had to be horse-crazy and had to help each other out. There was no rule regarding uniforms.

Now Stevie groaned. Lisa was neat and practical, as well as very smart, and because her mother was lesson-crazy, she'd learned to do all sorts of things. "Trust me, Lisa," Stevie said. "You don't need to embroider *anything*. Just as long as I don't have to be nice to Veronica." Not long ago they had all made New Year's resolutions. Lisa's was to learn embroidery, which she had—sort of. Stevie's was to be nice to Veronica, which she hadn't. Veronica was a horrid snob.

Veronica walked into the barn and down the aisle. "Did I hear you mention me, Stevie?" she asked, sticking her head in the stall door. "My, my, a committee meeting. Is there a reason you three are all in here while your horses are standing in the aisle?"

"Carole was just pointing out a section of Belle's windowsill that needs to be repainted,"

Stevie lied with great dignity. "And we couldn't help but admire your breeches. Did you get them at The Saddlery?"

Veronica laughed a tiny artificial laugh. "Oh, dear, of course not," she said. "You can't get these in stores. I had them custom made, and they cost a fortune! But they're great for the valentine season. Like the color? It's called cyclamen."

"Lovely," Lisa said. "Your legs look just like my mother's flowers."

Veronica looked as though she wasn't sure if this was a compliment. "Well, I'm off to fetch Danny," she said. Danny was her gorgeous Thoroughbred. "If you see Simon, tell him I'll be ready in a few minutes, okay?"

"Simon?" Stevie sputtered. Simon Atherton had been a geeky rider who had moved away from Willow Creek, Virginia, during what Stevie's mother would have referred to as his "awkward period of adolescence," and come back transformed into a total hunk.

"Of course," Veronica said sweetly. "We're going on a trail ride." She stroked the fluffy arm of her sweater. "My clothes are a little hint to get him to invite me to the Valentine's Day dance."

Veronica walked away toward Danny's stall.

4

The three members of The Saddle Club walked out to the aisle and watched her go. Lisa shook her head. "Now I've seen everything. She's a walking valentine."

The girls walked back into the aisle and Carole slumped against Starlight, her horse. "Custom made," she said disbelievingly, stroking the horse's back. "Stevie, you can't get those breeches in stores."

Stevie laughed. "Given Veronica's motive for wearing them, I'm not sure I'd want a pair. I mean, really!"

Lisa picked up a brush and began untangling Prancer's mane. Prancer was the Pine Hollow mare she usually rode. Lisa didn't have her own horse, but she loved Prancer. "I can't decide if I like them or not. I know they aren't traditional, Carole, but I think they're kind of fun. But if wearing pink breeches could attract Simon's attention—"

"Don't say it!" Stevie yelled. "Yuck! Lisa! How could you? I know he's gorgeous, but who cares? If he likes Veronica, there has to be something seriously wrong with his personality."

"I didn't say I would wear them," Lisa said. "I was going to say that if wearing pink breeches is

5

what it takes to attract Simon's attention, then maybe I wouldn't *want* to wear them."

"Oh, come on. He's not that bad, you guys. And he's not the first unsuspecting boy Veronica's sunk her hooks into," Carole objected. "He seems nice. Cute, too. Too bad he ignores us, even though I can hardly blame him, after the way we ignored him for years." She carefully brushed Starlight's ears. "It's hard to believe it's almost Valentine's Day already. I can't wait until the dance."

Every year, Max Regnery, the owner of Pine Hollow, put on a big Valentine's Day dance in the hay barn. It was always a lot of fun for all the kids and adults who rode at Pine Hollow.

"Eight days," Stevie said with satisfaction. "Eight days until my night of perfect romance." She batted her eyes dreamily and Carole and Lisa groaned. Stevie had a boyfriend named Phil Marsten. She wasn't usually dreamy about him, but then, a Valentine's Day dance was something special.

"I think the dance will be fun, but I don't think it will be romantic for me and Carole," Lisa said. Neither of them had boyfriends. "I wish there were *some* decent boys in Horse Wise." Horse

Wise was Pine Hollow's Pony Club. There were a lot of girls in it, a few very young boys, and some older boys who weren't showing any signs of Simon's miraculous transformation.

"Maybe you'll meet some cute guys from Cross County tomorrow," Stevie suggested. "I could get Phil to introduce you."

Carole and Lisa groaned again. Cross County was the Pony Club Phil belonged to. The next day the two clubs were meeting to practice mounted games for an upcoming competition.

"I'm not up for an instant boyfriend, thank you," Carole said. "Lisa and I will enjoy the dance on our own."

"We could invite everyone from Cross County, though," Lisa suggested. "Why not? I'll ask Max if we can." In addition to owning and running Pine Hollow, Max was the leader of Horse Wise.

"Sure," said Carole. "That's a good idea."

"Well, you can invite the whole club if you want to, but I've got a special invitation for Phil. I'm giving it to him tomorrow." Stevie turned slightly pink. "I made it."

"You made it?" Lisa asked. "You'll be doing embroidery next."

"Lisa, stop!" Carole scolded. "Stevie, that's nice. Phil will really like it."

"It's just a heart cut out of red construction paper," Stevie said. "But I really want this dance to be special." She dropped her brush into her grooming bucket. "Let's go ask Max now about inviting Cross County. He'll be teaching a lesson by the time we get back from our ride."

Lisa and Carole agreed. As they walked toward the stable office, the office door swung open and they heard Max say, "So if you don't mind, Mom, I'd really appreciate it if you'd handle the decorations for the dance."

"I'll be happy to do it," Max's mother replied. Her name was Mrs. Regnery, but she was always called Mrs. Reg, and she managed the stable for Max.

"Oh, good!" Carole said under her breath. Lisa and Stevie nodded. It was their private opinion that Mrs. Reg had not been herself lately. Late winter was always a gloomy time of year, but Mrs. Reg had seemed more distracted than anyone else at Pine Hollow. They hadn't heard her laugh for a week.

"What could be peppier than a bunch of bright

decorations?" Stevie said. "Plus, Mrs. Reg will do a great job. Phil will be really impressed!"

"I hope he'll pay more attention to you than to the decorations," Lisa said.

"Atmosphere is really important," Stevie said seriously.

"Hi, girls!" Max said, walking out the door and catching sight of them.

"Hi, Max!" they chorused. Just then, they heard Mrs. Reg laugh inside the office. Carole was relieved that Mrs. Reg was laughing—but surely the idea of decorating the hay barn hadn't pepped her up so quickly. Carole looked toward the door in puzzlement.

Max intercepted Carole's glance. "My mother's entertaining a new rider," he said. "Come in and meet him." He held the door open and the girls trooped inside.

A slender old man rakishly dressed in a cowboy hat and bolo tie was leaning against the corner of Mrs. Reg's desk. He had thin gray hair, a neat gray mustache, and bright blue eyes. When he saw the girls he straightened and politely tipped his hat to them. Max introduced the three members of The Saddle Club. "This is Mr. Stowe," he said to the girls. "He's our newest . . . rider."

Carole thought she heard a pause between *newest* and *rider*. Max looked faintly amused, too, and Carole thought she knew what these things meant. Old Mr. Stowe must not be much of a rider. He was certainly trying to look like one, though, with the cowboy hat and boots he was wearing. She felt sorry for him—he must not know that those things were meant for Western, not English, riding.

Mr. Stowe leaned back on Mrs. Reg's desk. "I was telling your boss here about the first dance I ever went on," he told them. "I swung my partner so hard I tripped her, and we both fell down!"

Mrs. Reg laughed. Max chuckled. Carole didn't understand what was funny. She'd die if some boy tripped her in the middle of a dance.

"I don't think we'll be doing any square dancing at our Valentine's Day dance," Lisa said politely.

"I hope not," Stevie said, less politely. "Phil and I—"

"Oh, well, times have changed," Mr. Stowe said. "Don't you agree, Mrs. Regnery?"

"Oh, please," Mrs. Reg said, "call me Elizabeth."

"Call me Howard," Mr. Stowe returned.

10

Max gave a small cough and started to leave. "Wait, Max!" called Lisa. She hurriedly asked him about Cross County. Max thought inviting the other Pony Club was a splendid idea.

"One other thing," Carole said, remembering something she had noticed earlier. "Dime is up here in the stall next to Starlight, where Mr. Anderson's horse used to be. Did somebody make a mistake, or has Dime's stall been changed?" Dime was one of the Pine Hollow lesson ponies. All the horses had permanently assigned stalls.

"Mr. Anderson built a stable on his property, so he took his horse home today," Max explained. "I moved Dime into that stall because it has a window low enough for him to look out of. I thought he'd like that."

"I bet he will," Carole said. "He's such a sociable little pony. I'm glad I asked, though, because I almost moved him back to his old stall when I saw him. I thought one of the little kids had made a mistake."

"Nope," Max said. "In fact, I'm moving Romeo into Dime's old stall. It's bigger than the one Dime has now, and Romeo's tall enough to look out the higher window." Romeo was Polly Giacomin's horse.

"Okay, Max. Thanks!" The girls said good-bye to Mrs. Reg and Mr. Stowe and returned to their horses.

"Geez!" said Lisa, as she picked the mud out of Prancer's hoof. "What was that Mr. Stowe about? Did you see the way he was bugging Mrs. Reg?"

"I can't believe she told him to call her Elizabeth," Stevie said. "I've never heard anyone call her anything but Mrs. Reg, except for Max and Deborah, and they call her Mom." Deborah was Max's wife.

"That Mr. Stowe can't be much of a rider," Carole said. She asked them if they, too, had noticed the odd tone in Max's voice.

"Yes, I did, but I don't think we should make assumptions just because he's so old," Lisa said. "Remember Dr. Dinmore?" The Saddle Club had once treated one of the best endurance riders in the country like a rank beginner because she was old.

"Don't remind me," Carole said. "I'm still embarrassed about that. But I'm not *entirely* saying he must be a beginner because he's old. Something in Max's voice wasn't quite right."

"Probably Max thinks he's a nuisance," Stevie declared. "I mean, all of us know better than to

12

stand around wasting Mrs. Reg's time. That would just give her more reason to put us to work."

Lisa and Carole laughed. Work was a Pine Hollow tradition. All the riders helped keep the stable clean and the horses cared for, and Mrs. Reg was widely known for her dislike of seeing any rider idle. Whenever she came across anyone who wasn't already working or riding, she put that person to work in short order.

"I adore Mrs. Reg," Carole said, "but I agree. I sure wouldn't want to be showing her how much free time I had."

"Who has free time?" Stevie asked. "What we've got now is riding time."

Lisa gave Prancer a pat. "And not a minute too soon!"

THE GIRLS PICKED up their grooming buckets and went to get their tack. On the way out of the tack room, they heard Mrs. Reg laugh again.

"I can't believe it!" Lisa muttered. "He's still in there bugging her."

Carole looked out the main door. "Max is teaching an adult lesson in the outdoor arena. Shouldn't Mr. Stowe be riding in it?" she whispered.

"Whatever he should be doing, he shouldn't be bothering Mrs. Reg," Stevie whispered back. "How can she concentrate on the dance decorations? He's probably telling her more stories about how clumsy he used to be."

Stevie clomped over to the office with her saddle over her arm and Belle's bridle hanging from her shoulder. She knocked on the open door. "Mr. Stowe!" she said. "We were just wondering if you wanted to . . ." Stevie paused. She couldn't think of a way to finish the sentence. What she was really wondering was how they could get Mr. Stowe to quit bothering Mrs. Reg. Stevie realized she should have consulted her friends before she opened her mouth. "Uh—" Stevie stammered.

"Yes?" Mrs. Reg asked. "What is it, Stevie?"

"We were wondering if Mr. Stowe wanted to go on a trail ride with us," Carole said smoothly. Lisa and Stevie looked at Carole wide-eyed. Carole narrowed her eyes at them. It wasn't her fault! Stevie had started it, and Carole had just finished her sentence in the only way that seemed both polite and possible.

"Please," Lisa added faintly.

Mr. Stowe looked tickled. "Well, certainly, ladies, thank you. I'd love to ride out with you— that is, Elizabeth, if you will join us." He swept off his hat and smiled at Mrs. Reg.

"But she has work to do!" Lisa blurted out. She thought Stevie was going a little overboard imagining Mrs. Reg's zeal for the dance decorations, but she knew how busy Mrs. Reg always was, and she didn't think it could be pleasant for her to have Mr. Stowe hanging around. It reminded her of the way Simon Atherton had trailed after them in his geek days.

Mr. Stowe and Mrs. Reg looked at each other. Both seemed a little uncomfortable.

"I certainly hope I haven't been disturbing you," Mr. Stowe said.

"Oh, no, not at all," Mrs. Reg said quickly.

"It is a lovely day for a trail ride," Mr. Stowe said. "If you'd care to . . ."

Mrs. Reg actually blushed a little. Carole was embarrassed for her. How dreadful of Mr. Stowe to make her feel so uneasy! "Ordinarily I would love to," Mrs. Reg said. "Any other day . . . but today, unfortunately, I do have to get this feed order finished. The feed store rep is coming at four o'clock—"

"And I've been distracting you." Mr. Stowe looked stricken.

"No, I've enjoyed it," Mrs. Reg protested, with what seemed to Lisa excessive but admirable politeness. "And it is a lovely day. Why don't you go out with the girls and enjoy yourself?"

16

Stevie had hoped that Mr. Stowe would just take the hint and leave Mrs. Reg alone. Unfortunately, both Mrs. Reg and Mr. Stowe seemed to take the trail ride offer seriously. Really! As if they would want to ride with Mr. Stowe! Still, Stevie knew the invitation was mostly her own fault. And at least if Mr. Stowe was with them, he wouldn't be annoying Mrs. Reg. It would be a noble sacrifice.

"Well, thank you, girls. It's a nice offer to make to an old man. I'm sure I'll have fun." Mr. Stowe smiled. "I haven't been out on the trails here yet, but Elizabeth assures me that they're lovely."

"They are," Carole said. "Uh—Mrs. Reg, what horse should he ride?"

Mrs. Reg thought for a moment. "You rode Nero on Wednesday, didn't you, Howard? I think Delilah would be a good mount for you on the trail. She's a lovely palomino."

Carole nodded. The names of both horses confirmed Carole's suspicions about Mr. Stowe's limited riding ability. Nero was a very old, gentle lesson horse who was about to be retired, but he was sometimes a little nervous out in the woods. Delilah was both gentle and ladylike, no matter

17

where she was. She would take good care of a beginning rider.

"We'll be careful with him, Mrs. Reg," Carole said, giving up her plans for galloping Starlight through the stubbled fields. "We won't jump or anything like that."

"Good," Mrs. Reg said briskly.

Mr. Stowe looked confused. "Just what would you be jumping?" he asked.

Carole was astounded. "The jumps," she said. "The jumps out on the trails." Surely Mr. Stowe couldn't be that ignorant!

"Oh, you mean the *horses* will be jumping," Mr. Stowe said. "I thought maybe you girls had some sort of preride ritual. I was hoping you wouldn't make me a part of it. My vertical leap, I'm sorry to say, has diminished considerably with age."

Mrs. Reg laughed again and none of the girls knew what to think. Stevie couldn't tell if Mr. Stowe was joking or serious. If he was joking, it was a pretty stupid joke, but if he was serious, they were in for an awful ride. Anyone who knew anything about English riding knew that the horses were taught to jump obstacles.

Lisa took a deep breath. "We'd better go," she said. "Our horses are waiting on the cross-ties."

18

Lisa knew Prancer would get impatient if she had to wait much longer.

"Have fun, all of you," Mrs. Reg said. "Have fun, Howard."

Stevie thought that she had never once in her life met a person named Howard. She tried to imagine Mr. Stowe as a baby named Howard, but couldn't. "We'll show you where Delilah is," she offered.

"We'll help you groom her and tack up," Carole continued. She doubted Mr. Stowe would know how to do any of this.

"Oh, I can manage that," Mr. Stowe said cheerfully. "Point me to my horse and point me to my gear, and I'll do the rest. You girls tend to your own horses. Christy, is it?"

"*Carole*," Carole corrected him.

"Carole, sorry," Mr. Stowe said. "And I'm riding Jemima."

"*Delilah*," Carole said. She felt a faint twinge of irritation. She sometimes struggled with people's names, but really, Jemima! She loved Delilah second only to Starlight, her own horse. She decided that she would have to keep a close eye on Mr. Stowe. Despite what he said, he might not know what he was doing. Carole didn't want De-

19

lilah to suffer from Mr. Stowe's ignorance. What if he twisted the girth, or didn't clean out Delilah's hooves? "I'll just go along with you," Carole offered.

Lisa and Stevie knew what Carole intended. They would all have to keep close watch on this man. Lisa took Carole's saddle from her and Stevie took her bridle, and they tacked up Starlight as well as their own horses. When they met at the mounting block outside the stable, however, Carole looked more cheerful.

"See," Mr. Stowe said, "I told you I knew how to do it. You didn't need to watch me after all."

"Yes, but I didn't know that," Carole replied.

Mr. Stowe grinned. "I know, and I don't blame you. Disreputable-looking character like me, you want to make sure I treat your horses right."

"You don't look disreputable!" Lisa protested. Mr. Stowe had exchanged his cowboy hat for the protective helmet Max insisted all riders wear. He still looked more Western than English with his cowboy boots, jeans, and bolo tie, but he didn't look disreputable—and besides, Stevie often rode in cowboy boots.

Mr. Stowe checked Delilah's girth, lowered his stirrups, and swung into the saddle with practiced grace. Carole breathed a sigh of relief, just as she had when she saw him curry Delilah in counter-clockwise circles and expertly untangle the straps of her bridle. He wasn't a total beginner, at least. She mounted Starlight. Stevie and Lisa mounted Belle and Prancer.

"Oh, I look disreputable enough next to you pretty girls," Mr. Stowe said. "Still, it's nice of you to have pity on an old man. I consider it a treat to be riding out with you."

Lisa thought it was no wonder Mrs. Reg had been laughing so much, if this was how Mr. Stowe usually talked.

"We weren't taking pity on you," Stevie told him. Carole coughed to keep from laughing. No, they weren't taking pity on Mr. Stowe. They were taking pity on Mrs. Reg.

Still, it was hard to dislike the old man. He actually seemed rather charming, in a pesky sort of way.

They started out on the easiest, flattest section of trail, and it was clear to all the girls that while Mr. Stowe was not an advanced rider, he was not a beginner, either. He rode more as if he were sitting in a chair than on a horse, and he let his shoulders slump and his heels come up, but he was relaxed and handled the reins competently and gently. After they'd walked a little while, he gave Delilah a pat. "Nice girl. She's got good gaits, doesn't she?" he said. "Like settin' in a rocking chair. Not as much of a looker as the three you all are riding, though. Carole, is yours a Thoroughbred?"

Carole warmed to Mr. Stowe. "No, Starlight's part Thoroughbred, but he's not a registered horse," she said. "He does look like a Thoroughbred, though. Prancer, the horse Lisa is riding, she's a Thoroughbred."

"I guessed that," Mr. Stowe said. "The tucked-up way she carries herself, and those long, elegant legs. I've always liked Thoroughbreds. They look kind of like ballerinas to me.

"Stevie, I can't place your mare," he continued. "She's got a nice shape and a pretty way of going, but I just don't know what breed she looks like. Nice little head, good ears."

Stevie smiled. "Belle's a combination—part Saddlebred and part Arabian."

Mr. Stowe smiled. "Oh, I should have known. That's a good blend."

All three girls were beginning to find Mr.

22

Stowe a remarkably pleasant man. "Which breed do you like best?" Lisa asked him.

He chuckled. "As I said, I like to look at Thoroughbreds. Every now and again I go to a racetrack and look at them all day long. But for me, riding, I want a nice horse with a nice comfortable trot and a good attitude. I don't care about breeds when I'm riding."

"That's great," Carole said enthusiastically. "That's the way I think everyone should feel. I've seen too many people get hung up on who a horse is or who his parents were. What's important is what a horse does."

They had ridden into the thick of the woods and now crossed a wide stream. Prancer picked her way delicately through the water, and Belle snorted at a dead leaf waving at the end of a branch. Starlight gave a playful jog. Delilah pricked her ears.

"When did you start riding?" Stevie asked Mr. Stowe.

"I never took it up seriously, the way I can see you kids do," he replied. "What happened was, I had an uncle who had horses. They were decent animals, kind, not fancy, and I used to go out and ride them all the time when I was a kid. I never had lessons, I just ran the horses around the fields. But I did enjoy it.

"After I grew up I didn't ride for years and years. Then I met Elizabeth—your Mrs. Reg—a few weeks ago, and my interest was rekindled."

"That's nice," Carole said. "Where did you meet Mrs. Reg? Was she advertising for new riding students? I know Pine Hollow had a few openings."

"No, she didn't say anything about the barn at first. I ran into her in that bookstore in Willow Creek, and we just sort of fell into a conversation. I go there pretty often. Turns out Mrs. Reg—Elizabeth—does, too. Pretty soon she was telling me about the horses, and so here I am."

Carole felt pleased for Mr. Stowe. She could never imagine herself not riding. How wonderful it must feel to him to be back on a horse after so long! And now, here at Pine Hollow, he could have all the opportunities for instruction that he'd been denied as a child. He could learn everything!

"You might try pushing your heels down a little," she suggested to him. "It would give you a better base of support."

24

"Yes, I see the way you three do it," he replied. "It looks mighty uncomfortable."

"It's much more comfortable when you get used to it," Lisa assured him. Like Carole, she was beginning to feel an interest in Mr. Stowe's education. "You know, I haven't been riding for very long. The instruction here at Pine Hollow is really good."

"Well, fine," Mr. Stowe said amiably. He stuck his heels down, and even if they did come up again a few strides later, Carole gave him points for trying.

"There's one of the jumps," Stevie said, pointing to a pile of logs leading into an open field. "You asked before what we jumped. That's a jump."

Mr. Stowe asked Delilah to halt and looked at it closely. "So that's a jump, eh? And the horses jump it, not the riders?"

Once again Stevie wasn't sure whether Mr. Stowe was kidding. "We both jump it," she said uncertainly, "together."

"Or not together, depending," Lisa said with a snort, remembering the times she'd come off Prancer in midair.

"I'll tell you what," Mr. Stowe said. "I'd sure

love to watch you ladies take that jump. I'd know more what you were talking about then. Maybe you could all jump it a couple of times, just for me? As a favor?"

"Sure!" Stevie couldn't see why Mr. Stowe would want to stand still while they jumped—and from his grin she almost believed that he really was teasing them—but she had been dying to jump Belle. She led the way, and Carole and Lisa followed.

When they had jumped the fence several times in both directions, Mr. Stowe thanked them gravely. They rode back to Pine Hollow. On the way home they passed several more jumps, and at Mr. Stowe's request The Saddle Club jumped them all.

When they got back Mrs. Reg was waiting for them. "The girls' horses look considerably more winded than yours," she observed to Mr. Stowe. "I hope they didn't abandon you."

Mr. Stowe dismounted and explained about the jumping demonstrations. Mrs. Reg smiled. "I'll help you put Delilah away," she offered. She took the reins from his hands.

"You don't need to, Mrs. Reg!" Carole assured her. "He really does a fine job."

Mrs. Reg smiled—not at Carole, but at Mr. Stowe. "I'll help him anyway," she said.

Once the three Saddle Club members were alone, Carole shook her head. "Mrs. Reg just doesn't trust him," she said.

"You can't blame her, can you?" Lisa asked. "After all, we didn't trust him, either, until you watched him tack up. You know, he really is a nice old man, even if he is a little strange."

"We'll have to teach him things," Carole said. "I just think it's so great that he's able to ride again. It must be like a dream come true."

"I don't mind teaching him around the stable," Stevie said. "And I agree, Lisa, that he is a really nice old man. But let's not take him on trail rides again, okay?"

"Why not? It wasn't that bad. We still got to jump."

Stevie grinned. "I couldn't talk about Phil!"

Lisa looked at Carole and laughed. "Remember that," she said. "If Stevie's Valentine's Day attitude gets too oppressive to those of us without boyfriends, we'll just make sure to take Mr. Stowe with us."

Carole agreed. "He'll be our Valentine's Day antidote," she said. "Our anti-valentine."

THE NEXT MORNING Horse Wise met at Pine Hollow and then traveled to Cross County for the mounted games practice. The Pony Clubs held several different competitions each year, including games, which were relay races on horseback. This meeting with Cross County was only a practice, but of course everyone from Horse Wise wanted to do well. "*Well*," Stevie explained, "as in 'better than Cross County.'"

Lisa and Carole rolled their eyes. Colonel Hanson, Carole's father, was driving them, along with Meg Durham and Betsy Cavanaugh, to Cross County. Meg and Betsy were sitting in the very back of the Hansons' station wagon, whispering.

Finally Betsy said, "Okay, great," and Meg turned around.

"Is it okay if I'm on your team today?" Meg asked The Saddle Club. Teams were made of four riders.

"If Max lets us pick teams, sure," Lisa answered. "But don't you want to be on Veronica's team?" Meg and Betsy were both Veronica's friends more than they were The Saddle Club's friends.

Meg made a face. "See, Veronica asked Simon Atherton to be on her team."

"And she kicked you off?" Stevie said. "That's despicable!"

"No," Meg said, "but we know both Betsy and I can't be on her team—I mean, Adam's on it, too, and Betsy—well . . ." Meg paused; Betsy blushed.

"Betsy likes Adam," Carole supplied. She'd guessed that already.

"I'm hoping he'll ask me to the Valentine's Day dance," Betsy confided.

"Besides," Meg said confidently, "I think any team with you three on it is more likely to win than any team full of lovebirds."

"Thanks," Carole said. "But Stevie here, she's a lovebird herself."

Stevie smiled and fingered the red heart-shaped invitation she was bringing for Phil. "It's different with us," she said. "I mean, we're an established couple. I know Phil will want to go to the dance with me."

As soon as they arrived on the Cross County grounds, Stevie jumped out of the car. Lisa and Carole followed more slowly, heading for the horse van Max had brought from Pine Hollow. They could see Phil detach himself from a group of Cross County riders and hurry toward Stevie with a big smile on his face.

"Uh-oh," Lisa said. "Is that an invitation in Phil's hand?"

Carole looked and nodded. "Trouble," she said.

A moment later they could hear Stevie's shriek carried back to them on the wind: "What do you *mean* you don't want to go to my dance?"

Stevie stomped back to the rest of The Saddle Club. "I've never been so disgusted in my entire life," she said. She threw a piece of red paper on the ground.

Lisa automatically bent down and retrieved it. "Is this your invitation?" she asked.

"No," said Stevie. "I mean, yes. I mean, it's

Phil's invitation to me. His school is having a Valentine's Day dance, and he actually wants me to go to that instead of him coming to Pine Hollow."

"Go to both," Carole suggested.

"I can't!" wailed Stevie. "They're on the same night, at the same time. I told Phil I thought we'd have a much better time at Pine Hollow, especially since Max is inviting Cross County, but Phil is on the committee for his school dance. He says he's been working really hard to make his dance nice, so he wants to go to that one."

"That sounds reasonable," Lisa said. "We'll miss you, but I bet you'll still have fun."

"But I don't want to go to his dance! At some school where I don't know anyone! Plus, I won't be around you guys. Plus, I want Phil to come to our dance. I was really planning on a special night for us. His school dance just wouldn't be the same."

"Girls," Max called, "I could use your help here." He was beginning to unload the Pine Hollow horses from the trailer.

Actually, Carole corrected herself, Max was beginning to unload the Pine Hollow *ponies* from the trailer: Quarter, Nickel, Dime, and Penny.

The games were relays, so they only needed one mount per team, and the ponies were much easier for the little kids to ride than the horses, especially since relay games involved so much mounting and dismounting.

They divided into ten teams, four from Pine Hollow and six from Cross County. "We've got to beat Phil's team," Stevie said urgently as they saddled Dime, their team's mount.

"I don't think that will make him more likely to come to our dance," Lisa pointed out. She tightened Dime's girth another notch. Dime turned his head as if to nip her. Lisa pulled firmly on his far rein to straighten his head. It wasn't like Dime to be naughty.

Stevie glared at Lisa. "It's a matter of principle," she said.

Lisa sighed. Stevie was known for her competitive streak—and so was Phil.

"We'll do our best," Carole said soothingly.

Stevie brightened. "And our best is pretty good."

HOWEVER, THE DAY did not go well for anyone from Pine Hollow. The first race was the flag race. One by one, each rider on each team had to trot or canter up to a wooden stand, insert a flag in it, and race to the finish line to hand over the pony to the next rider. Once all four flags were flying, the team members had to do the same thing backward, taking the flags out one at a time.

Penny, a Pine Hollow pony, was being ridden by a team of young but good riders: Matthew, Jasmine, May, and Corey. Matthew rode first. He grabbed a flag and urged Penny into a trot. Penny took off at a flying gallop. She ran past the flag stand, ran past the finish line on the other end of the playing field, and galloped madly out into the open field beyond that.

Matthew shouted at Penny and tried vainly to slow her down. Max shouted instructions to him. Eventually Matthew got Penny turned—and the mare galloped back the other way, across the finish line, past the flag stand, across the starting line, and through the field on the other side.

All the other horses were made nervous by Penny's galloping. Most of the other teams stopped their horses until Matthew managed to halt Penny. The little boy looked fiercely angry. "She's not listening to me!" he said.

33

"I can see that," Max said gently. "It's not your fault. Try starting out at the walk, and see how she does."

Matthew kept Penny at a tight-reined walk and finally got his flag in his team's stand. He handed Penny over to Jasmine. Jasmine mounted, and Penny took off with Jasmine across the field.

Next Penny took off with Corey and then with May. By then the entire game was in an uproar. Jasmine was in tears because she was furious. Jessica Adler, a little girl on another team, was in tears because she loved Penny. Worse yet, all of the Cross County riders were laughing.

Stevie was riding Dime, who seemed upset by Penny's antics. He was refusing to obey any of Stevie's directions. When Stevie told Dime to turn left, he tried to turn right. Stevie had ridden the pony many times before, and she had never known him to be quarrelsome.

"This is a disaster," Lisa moaned.

"Tell me about it," Stevie said, gritting her teeth. She pushed Dime across the finish line and held him while Lisa mounted. Just then Max called for a time-out.

"Let's stop and get reorganized," Max said. He held the side of Penny's bridle with one hand, and with the other he patted Jasmine's shoulder. "Carole, could you come here?"

Carole went to Max's side.

"Take Penny out in that field and teach her a lesson," Max said quietly. "Make her walk, make her trot, and then make her canter until she wants to trot. Make her listen to you. She's got to start behaving before she hurts one of these kids."

"Of course, Max," Carole said. She adjusted Penny's stirrups so that they would fit her longer legs. She felt proud that Max had chosen her. Of course, he was too big to ride Penny, or he probably would have schooled her himself. But Carole knew how important it was that Penny not get away with her bad behavior. Every pony had a bad day once in a while, but usually Penny was very good-natured, so Carole felt sure she would get over her problem soon.

Carole mounted and gathered up the reins. She made Penny walk slowly until they were well away from the playing field and could no longer bother the other horses. She made her walk in two tight circles, one in each direction. She made her walk a slow circuit of the open field.

She could feel Penny's resistance—the mare still didn't want to be good. Carole pushed her into a trot. She would trot and then canter, just as Max had said.

Penny had other ideas. As soon as Carole told her to go forward, she took off like a miniature rocket. Carole pulled hard on the reins, but the bit Penny wore was mild and she ignored it entirely. Penny galloped for the far side of the field as fast as she could, and when she got there she spun around and galloped back. Carole nearly fell off when Penny wheeled. She grabbed a handful of Penny's mane and fought to keep her balance. Suddenly they were almost back at the playing field! Carole knew she couldn't let Penny rush across it once more. She pulled on the left rein with all her might, and Penny turned and galloped across the field again.

They went back and forth like a bumper car out of control. Carole fought to keep her balance and to slow Penny. In the end, when Penny dropped to a walk, Carole was so out of breath she was almost dizzy. Her arms hurt from trying to control the stupid pony.

"Make her canter again," Max commanded.

"I can't," Carole whispered to herself, but she had never said that to Max, not once, and she had vowed she never would. She turned Penny and grimly cantered her the length of the field. Penny stretched out her nose, grabbed the bit in her teeth, and tried to run again. Carole hauled her back.

When she returned to the playing field, everyone except Lisa, Stevie, and Max looked ready to burst from smothered laughter.

"That's some feisty pony," one of the Cross County riders said, and the whole Cross County club exploded with laughter.

Even Jasmine was giggling. "Thank you, Carole," she said. "I don't feel so bad about not being able to ride her if *you* can't."

Carole's face was flushed and her eyes were dark with anger and shame. Stevie could imagine how humiliated Carole felt. Penny was being a beast, and that wasn't Carole's fault; and Stevie knew that even the smallest ponies were physically stronger than any rider, but still, this had to be a huge blow to Carole's pride.

Stevie started to walk toward her friend when behind her she heard Lisa shriek, "Dime! You *brat!*"

Stevie whirled just in time to see Dime leap into the air and perform a truly impressive series of bucks. Lisa fought to get his head up so that he couldn't use it to counterbalance his flying heels, but within seconds she was sitting on the ground and Dime was flying toward the same open field Penny had frolicked in moments before.

Penny plunged and whirled, trying to join him. Carole hung on to the reins grimly. Max grabbed Penny's bridle and soothed the excited mare. "Lisa, are you hurt?" he called.

Lisa was already on her feet, dusting off the seat of her breeches. "No," she answered. From the tone of her voice, her friends knew she was as angry and humiliated as Carole. Every rider fell off occasionally, but to be bucked off by the gentlest pony in the barn, in front of a huge audience of kids your own age—that was special.

"I'll go get him, Max," Lisa said. She wanted to get away from the other riders, if only for a moment. She hadn't been this embarrassed since the first week she started riding, when Stevie had played a practical joke on her. Angry tears came to her eyes.

"Thank you, Lisa," Max said gently. Unlike Penny, Dime had stopped galloping at the farthest edge of the field. He was now eating grass as though he didn't have a care in the world—or a saddle on his back. Lisa walked slowly toward him. She knew better than to rush at any horse, but she also wanted to give herself time to regain her composure. *At least when I get back my face won't be red anymore,* she thought.

Dime cocked a wary ear toward her. Lisa slowed her steps even more. "Whoa, Dime," she said softly. "Good pony. Steady, good boy." Dime relaxed his ear and continued grazing. "Stupid moronic pea-brain," Lisa crooned, in the same gentle tone. "Fluff-headed idiot."

Dime relaxed still further. Lisa gave a small snort of laughter. Max had always told them that horses couldn't understand English. Now she knew it was true.

Dime's reins were still looped around his neck. Lisa cautiously went up to his side and reached for them.

Dime leaped sideways. Lisa's fingers closed on empty air, and Dime galloped, bucking and plunging, all the way back to the playing field. Fortunately, Carole had already dismounted from Penny, and she and Stevie managed to catch him.

Max called another time-out while he consulted with the Cross County leader. Finally he put both Penny and Dime back on the horse van. Horse Wise borrowed a horse from Cross County, and the riders reorganized themselves into eight teams of five. Polly joined Veronica's team, Jackie went to Penny's old team, and a rider named Liam joined one of the Cross County teams. Jessica Adler joined The Saddle Club and Meg.

Jessica was still upset over Penny's misbehavior. "She was awful," she said. "And I love her so much. Why would she be so bad?"

"Maybe she isn't feeling well," Carole suggested. "We'll check her when we get back to Pine Hollow." Personally she believed Penny felt fine. Any pony who galloped that much could hardly be sick.

"Maybe she just woke up on the wrong side of the stall," Lisa suggested, putting her arm around the little girl.

Phil brought a big ugly gray horse over to them. "Here, you guys can ride Joker," he said. "Don't worry, he won't run away with you. He can't move that fast." Phil flashed a devilish smile at all of them and returned to his team.

"Maybe Penny's got a brat of a boyfriend who wants to get his own way all the time," Stevie spat. "Maybe she's just really tired of putting up with him."

"Stevie!" Lisa said.

Stevie looked at her friends. They were having a bad day, too. "I'm sorry," she said. "Jessica, try not to worry about Penny. I'm sure she'll be her own nice self the next time you ride her. Meanwhile, let's give old Joker a try."

Meg looked at Joker critically. "I bet this old horse couldn't gallop if he wanted to," she said. "We're not going to win a thing."

They never found out if Joker could gallop or not. Only Carole could even convince him to canter. They did discover, however, just how the horse had got his name. In the flag race, as soon as Stevie had put her flag in the stand, Joker reached back and pulled it out with his teeth. In the spoon race he flipped his head right before the finish line, and the egg broke all over Jessica's breeches. And in the balloon-popping race he actually popped a balloon with his hoof. Max had to disqualify their team.

"It wasn't just the horse," Carole said with a groan on the drive back to Pine Hollow. "We weren't exactly stellar riders, either."

"Don't remind me," Lisa said. She'd gotten tangled in a clown suit during the costume race and had fallen off again when she'd tried to dismount. "Twice in one day. Aargh."

"At least you were *trying* to dismount the second time," Stevie said. "You just dismounted a little faster than you'd planned. Everybody in Cross County saw me miss my balloon." She'd had to circle around and try again.

In the back of the station wagon, Betsy giggled. "I've never seen you guys have so much trouble. Jessica was the best rider on your team."

"Thanks," Meg said shortly.

"Sorry," Betsy said to her friend. "But it was funny, really. Veronica and Simon were so busy trying to show off for one another that they both rode really well. Adam did a pretty nice job, too. You've got to admit, he looks pretty good on a horse."

Carole and Lisa rolled their eyes at one another. Betsy had to be smitten to consider Adam attractive.

"He sure does look better on a horse," Stevie said. "When he's wearing a riding helmet, you can hardly see his face."

Betsy and Meg lapsed into sullen silence. The Saddle Club did, too. No one spoke until they pulled up at Pine Hollow and got out of the car. Then Stevie said, "Oh, no! Will you look at that!"

"What?" asked Lisa.

Stevie pointed to the office window. "That Mr. Stowe! He's in there bugging Mrs. Reg again!"

THE SADDLE CLUB stared. There indeed was Mr. Stowe, standing in the open office doorway talking to Mrs. Reg.

"She'll never get the dance decorations planned at this rate," Stevie muttered. "Not that it matters, if Phil can't bother to come."

"It matters to us," Lisa replied sharply. Her hip was sore from falling off Dime, and she was getting sick of Stevie's complaining. "We might not have boyfriends, but we'd still like to have a decent time."

"Oh, really!" Carole sounded exasperated. "As if Mr. Stowe talking to Mrs. Reg for five minutes is going to mess up the Valentine's Day dance!"

"He may have been bugging her for *hours*," Stevie pointed out.

Carole couldn't decide whether or not she truly believed Mr. Stowe was making a nuisance of himself. On the one hand, Mrs. Reg looked pretty cheerful. On the other hand, she always complained when students, even adult students, wasted their time gossiping when they had work to do.

"You're right," she said to Stevie grimly. "We'll have to do something about him."

Max pulled up with the horse trailer. Behind him, Veronica, Simon, and Adam piled out of the diAngelos' Mercedes. Veronica waved her fingers airily at The Saddle Club. "So sorry none of you could control those ponies today," she trilled. "Was teeny little Penny just a bit much for you, Carole?"

Carole pressed her lips together. "Come on," she said to her friends, ignoring Veronica, "let's help Max unload."

"I really think you ought to let us do that," Veronica suggested. "Given the way games practice went for your team, you've probably done enough with the ponies. Dime might get away from one of you and run all the way back to Cross

County. Why don't you all clean their tack?" She looked at Simon admiringly. "Simon can unload the ponies. He's so nice and strong."

"Forget it," Stevie said, starting forward. "If you think—"

"Stevie." Lisa pulled at Stevie's jacket. "Let's do what she says."

"I'm not giving her the satisfaction," Stevie said. "Dime running away from us! Give me a break! We can do some things right."

Carole agreed with Lisa. "Nothing's gone right today so far. And anyway, if we're in the tack room, we can't see Veronica laughing at us."

"Besides," Lisa said, "my hip is sore. I'd like to sit down. And if I don't see that rotten Dime again for a week, I won't be sorry."

Stevie gave in. "At least after we clean the ponies' tack, we can take our own horses out on a trail ride," she suggested. The others agreed gladly. After the morning they'd had, they needed a trail ride.

They took the ponies' sweat-soaked saddles and bridles out of the cab of Max's truck and carried them into the stable. On the way to the tack room they passed Mrs. Reg's office. Mr. Stowe still stood in the open doorway. Apparently he had been telling jokes, because when they walked by they heard him say, "And what about this one: How many psychologists does it take to change a lightbulb?"

Stevie stopped to listen. She liked dumb jokes.

"Only one," said Mr. Stowe. "But the lightbulb has to really want to change."

Mrs. Reg laughed, but Stevie didn't understand what was funny. She felt a wave of annoyance wash over her. How was Mrs. Reg ever going to take care of the dance decorations with this old man telling pointless jokes all day? "Mr. Stowe, why don't you come with us," she said abruptly. "We're going to clean tack."

Mr. Stowe turned and smiled. "Why, hello, Stevie, Carole, Lisa," he said. "How nice to see you again. Did you have a nice time at Cross Country? Elizabeth told me you were playing games with them."

"It's Cross *County*," Stevie corrected. "And we were playing games *against* them, not *with* them."

"And we didn't have a very nice time," Lisa added, thinking that Stevie's fierce tone required some explanation. She told them about Dime's and Penny's awful behavior.

"How strange," Mrs. Reg commented. To Mr.

Stowe she added, "Normally they're both very sweet and dependable."

"So now we're cleaning the tack we used," Stevie said. "Come on, Mr. Stowe. You can help us."

Mr. Stowe smiled gently. "I wouldn't be much help, I'm afraid. As far as I remember, my uncle didn't clean his tack at all—at least not while I was around. I don't know the first thing about it."

"We'll show you," Carole said. "It's not hard, but it is important. Mrs. Reg's always telling us so, aren't you, Mrs. Reg? You're supposed to clean your tack after each ride."

"Didn't you clean Delilah's bridle yesterday?" Lisa asked.

Mr. Stowe looked embarrassed. "Well, no—"

"I guess it's not that important," Lisa said hurriedly. She turned to Mrs. Reg. "I mean, I know it is, Mrs. Reg, but I don't think you should get upset with Mr. Stowe. He just didn't know."

"That's okay, Lisa, I'm not upset," Mrs. Reg said gently.

"I'm very sorry," Mr. Stowe said in confusion. "I didn't realize. If I was supposed to clean tack, then I'd better start cleaning. Thank you, Carole.

I'll accept your kind offer." He tipped his hat to Mrs. Reg, took one of the two bridles Carole was carrying, and accompanied The Saddle Club to the tack room.

They had to teach Mr. Stowe everything. It turned out he didn't even know how to take apart a bridle! "I just never messed with this stuff before," he said apologetically. "But it's important to Elizabeth, eh?"

"Very important," Carole said firmly. She showed him how to open the tab buckles that fastened the reins to the bit. "In the first place, salt from a horse's sweat can damage the leather, and tack is expensive, so you want it to last. In the second place, it's healthier for the horses if everything is kept clean and supple. And in the third place, it just looks nicer. Mrs. Reg likes everything neat and clean."

"Runs a tidy ship, does she?" he asked. "I thought so. Everything around here seems brushed and raked and straightened. Still, I wouldn't call her too neat—not *too* fastidious— would you?" He looked around at all of them.

Lisa thought about the question as she removed the stirrups from Dime's saddle and dunked them into a pail of water. "She's not afraid of getting dirty, if that's what you mean," she answered. "But Mrs. Reg really likes everything done right. That's her job, you know—she manages the stable for Max." Lisa put saddle soap on a sponge and began cleaning Dime's saddle. Stevie did the same with Nickel's. Carole dismantled Quarter's bridle.

"Mr. Stowe!" Carole shrieked. "Don't do that!"

Mr. Stowe froze. Delilah's bit hung from his hand, just above Stevie's bucket of soapy water. Stevie redirected him to Lisa's bucket of clean water. "Don't ever put soap on a horse's bit," Carole explained. "It'll taste terrible!"

"Sorry," Mr. Stowe said. He took a sponge and began wiping off Delilah's reins. "So, what else can you tell me about Elizabeth?"

All three girls looked blank. "Oh!" said Lisa. "You mean Mrs. Reg!" Mr. Stowe nodded. "Well, she taught me how to do a lot of things around the stable: clean stalls and scrub water buckets, clean tack, mix horse feeds—"

"She keeps us all busy," Carole explained. "Everyone works at Pine Hollow."

"You told me," said Mr. Stowe. "But what is she like as a person?"

The Saddle Club looked blank again. "She tells

stories," Lisa said after a pause. "We usually think they don't have a point, but they usually do."

"She's a very *good* stable manager," Carole offered.

"She's a good rider, too," Stevie said. "And she arranges lots of the fun stuff we do here, too. Like, for instance, right now she's supposed to be planning the decorations for the Valentine's Day dance."

"I saw the sign on the bulletin board for the dance," Mr. Stowe said. "It's next Saturday, isn't it? Are you all going?"

"Of course we're going," Stevie said. "It's who might not be going that's upsetting me." She pressed her lips together and bent over Nickel's saddle, scrubbing furiously.

Lisa wondered what Mr. Stowe would think of Stevie's somewhat cryptic comment. Of course Mr. Stowe wouldn't know about Phil.

"Isn't Mrs. Reg going?" asked Mr. Stowe.

"She has to go," Carole said. "She manages the stable."

Mr. Stowe grinned. "I know. You told me."

"She always goes to stuff," Lisa said. "But she usually doesn't dance or anything like that. I don't think she likes parties, but she's always a

51

good sport about them. But anybody can come to the Valentine's Day dance. Max never minds who we invite."

"I see," said Mr. Stowe. "Do you think Mrs. Reg will invite anyone?"

Lisa frowned. "Who would she invite? All her friends are right here."

"Mr. Stowe," Carole said with a sigh, "you've got way too much lather on your sponge. Let me show you."

WHEN THEY WERE finished, Mr. Stowe stopped outside Delilah's stall and fed her a carrot. "I forgot to bring one yesterday," he explained to the girls as he gave Delilah a pat. "She's a good horse, though, isn't she? I always did prefer blondes." He chuckled.

"Mr. Stowe," Carole said, "Delilah isn't blond. She's palomino."

He smiled. "That's another thing I never did learn—all those fancy names for what colors horses are. To me, it's easy. You've got your brown horses, black ones, redheads, blonds, and white ones."

The three girls stared at him. "It's not as easy as

that," Lisa said, remembering how she'd struggled to learn all the correct terms.

"Horses aren't white at all," Stevie said. "You're supposed to call them *gray*."

"Now, see, that doesn't make sense," Mr. Stowe argued. "They don't look gray. They look white."

"It does make sense, and there are white horses," Carole cut in. "I'll show you." She led the way down the aisle to Sachia, a gray mare being boarded there. "Most white-haired horses are gray, or even black, when they're born, and they get lighter with age," she said. She carefully parted a section of Sachia's hair so that the mare's skin showed. "And see? She's got black skin. Nearly all horses have black skin. But every once in a while a horse is born with white hair at birth, and totally pink skin, and that's a white horse. They're very rare."

"I didn't know that," Stevie said, becoming interested. "Belle's got pink skin under her white markings."

"Yes," said Carole. "That's very common, but I bet she's got black skin everywhere else. Now, Mr. Stowe, I'll teach you the difference between a brown horse and a liver chestnut."

Mr. Stowe looked uncomfortable. "I wouldn't want to trouble you girls further," he said. "Why, Elizabeth! Is there something I can help you with?"

Mrs. Reg had come out of the office and was looking at her watch anxiously. "My car is in the shop, and Max took off with the truck," she said. "And Deborah must have the other car. I need to get some liniment from the tack shop before it closes. I'm afraid I won't make it." She sounded flustered.

"I'll take you," Mr. Stowe said instantly. He waved his thanks to the girls and left with Mrs. Reg.

"Well, honestly," said Carole. "I can't tell if he wants to learn about horses or not. Sometimes he just doesn't seem interested."

THEY GOT THEIR horses ready and headed for the trails. Once she was astride Prancer, Lisa felt the tensions of the morning melt away. "This is so much better," she said.

"I know," Carole said. "I don't think Starlight will run away with me."

Lisa snorted. "I bet you didn't think Penny was

54

going to run away with you, either," she said. Carole burst out laughing.

"I just can't believe that Phil!" Stevie cut in angrily. "Who does he think he is, not wanting to come to my party? I can't believe he'd miss a night of perfect romance because of some stupid committee. He's a snake! I never realized it before, but he truly is a snake."

"He's got a right to want to go to his own dance," Carole said. She could see Phil's side of the argument, and it seemed as valid as Stevie's. "You can't really blame him for not coming to Pine Hollow."

"I can too," Stevie retorted. "I'm going to help him make up his mind. He comes to Pine Hollow—or else."

ON SUNDAY AFTERNOON Lisa was riding her bicycle into Pine Hollow's driveway just as Carole was walking up. Carole often took the bus from her house to a stop near the stable and walked the rest of the way.

"Hi, Lisa," she called as Lisa parked her bike. "How's your hip?"

"Fine," Lisa said, smiling. "My ego is better, too. How's yours?"

Carole shook her head and laughed. "Still a little sore. That Penny!"

"Today it'll just be Starlight, Belle, and Prancer," Lisa said happily. "I can't wait to hit those trails." They'd planned to meet Stevie and ride together.

As they headed into the stable, they could hear that Stevie was already there. "But Mrs. Reg," came Stevie's voice from inside the office, "a live band would be so much better than just playing CDs on Max's stereo system. It would make the dance really special. Couldn't we at least get a band?"

Carole and Lisa walked into the office. Mrs. Reg and Stevie both smiled at them. "No," Mrs. Reg said firmly to Stevie. "We can't get a live band, we can't rent a strobe light, and for heaven's sake, we certainly can't get a laser light show. This is a barn dance, Stevie. It's not Madison Square Garden. Our budget will cover balloons and streamers, and that's about it."

"But everyone has balloons and streamers," Stevie wailed. "I want our dance to be spectacular."

Carole looked at Lisa and rolled her eyes. It was clear that Stevie wanted a spectacular show because she wanted to lure Phil away from his school dance. Carole didn't think this would work at all. In fact, though she more or less supported

Stevie because she knew how much the Pine Hollow dance meant to her, she also thought Phil had a good reason for not wanting to come. She knew they were both stubborn, and she hoped they wouldn't get into an awful fight over this.

"If you want spectacular, Stevie, you'll have to make it spectacular by the shining light of your personality," Mrs. Reg said firmly, with an amused glint in her eye.

"Good morning!" Mr. Stowe said cheerfully, coming into the room without knocking. He checked his watch. "Or I should say, good afternoon! I'm not interrupting anything important, am I?"

"No, I think Stevie was just finishing," Mrs. Reg said.

"I hope you're not expecting to ride today," Stevie told him. "Most of the horses get Sunday off." She couldn't believe he was here again! Would the old man never go away? He didn't seem horse-crazy enough to be hanging around Pine Hollow the way he was doing. *He must lead a very boring life*, decided Stevie.

"Stevie, you know that's not true," Mrs. Reg chided. To Mr. Stowe she added, "We do, of course, give every horse one day off a week, but never all at the same time." She smiled. "I know of two particular horses who could stand some exercise. Perhaps you would care to go on a trail ride with me?"

"But you've hardly gotten started planning the dance decorations!" Stevie protested. "They're very important!"

Mrs. Reg looked a trifle harassed. "I'll have plenty of time to do them, Stevie. They won't take that long."

"They should," Stevie muttered sulkily.

"Say," Mr. Stowe said cheerfully, "aren't you girls riding today? You'd better be getting those horses ready—don't want to miss any of this fine sunshine!" He took his cowboy hat off and laid it on Mrs. Reg's desk. Carole took this as a sign that he meant to stick around. She thought about how this must annoy Mrs. Reg.

"We're not riding, we're giving our horses the day off," Carole said.

Stevie looked apoplectic. "We *are?*" The Saddle Club did give their horses at least one day off a week, but usually that was Monday, the day they often volunteered at a therapeutic riding center, or else another weekday when they had appointments or schoolwork or something. It was never a weekend, when they were free to ride.

"Yes," said Carole firmly. "We came here to work. To clean stalls."

Lisa could see why Carole had said that—she was trying to distract Mr. Stowe—but she wondered what Mrs. Reg would think about her wearing clean breeches and knee boots to clean stalls in.

Mrs. Reg didn't seem to notice Lisa's clothes. Her face had lit up at Carole's declaration. "Wonderful!" she said. "We won't keep you. Red can tell you which stalls to clean."

Mr. Stowe looked surprised at the sudden change in Mrs. Reg's expression. "Everyone works at Pine Hollow, don't they?" he said. "Well, I'm eager to do my fair share. I can ride another day. I'll clean some stalls, too!"

"You certainly don't have to—" Mrs. Reg began.

"No, I'm happy to," Mr. Stowe said. He put his hat back on.

"We'll go get the wheelbarrows and find out which stalls to clean," Carole said. She grabbed Stevie and Lisa by the elbows and propelled them out of the office.

"I can't believe you said we weren't riding,"

Lisa grumbled. "Clean stalls! As if we haven't cleaned enough all week! And our horses don't need the day off! If anything, Prancer could use the exercise!"

"It worked, didn't it?" Carole answered. "Mr. Stowe is staying with us. Poor Mrs. Reg is being totally annoyed by him, and she shouldn't have to go out on a trail ride with him. Did you see how she was dressed? In that nice blouse and her good riding jacket? If she went out in the woods, she'd get all messed up!"

"Maybe she wanted to ride," Stevie said. "I know I did."

Lisa sighed. "No, Carole's probably right. I mean, I'm sure Mrs. Reg would have enjoyed a trail ride, but not with Mr. Stowe."

"Yeah," Stevie agreed. "He'd probably tell her lightbulb jokes the whole time. She'd be miserable."

"Still, I can't believe you said we weren't riding," Lisa said. "You could at least have said that we were riding after we cleaned stalls. Something."

"I can't believe Mrs. Reg didn't like my ideas for the dance," Stevie said. "A laser light show would have been really cool."

Carole laughed. "I can't believe that after spending yesterday showing Mr. Stowe how to clean tack, we're going to have to show him how to clean stalls, too."

IT TURNED OUT Mr. Stowe did know one end of a pitchfork from the other. "My uncle might not have cleaned his saddles too often, but he kept his horses' stalls in shape," he said cheerfully. "I was shoveling manure thirty-five years before any of you were born. Point me to the right stalls, ladies, and I'll show you and Elizabeth a thing or two about work."

Lisa had to admire his attitude. She wasn't feeling nearly so perky. She gave Prancer an apologetic pat before moving her to the cross-ties.

Red had assigned them all stalls in the front portion of the stable. Mr. Stowe did Calypso's stall in record time, and Carole, checking it, couldn't help admiring the neat, fluffy mound of fresh bedding. He had done a thorough job, fast.

"Hey!" Mr. Stowe shouted. The girls came running. He was standing in Dime's stall, holding the pony by his halter. "Durn pony tried to kick me," he said. "Nearly succeeded, too."

"Dime!" Lisa scolded. "What's gotten into you?"

"I've got him now," Mr. Stowe said. "It's okay." He put Dime on the cross-ties in the aisle and started on his stall, and the girls went back to work.

A few minutes later Mr. Stowe came to the door of Starlight's stall, where Carole was just finishing up. "I want to show you something," he said. Carole followed him back to Dime's stall, and Mr. Stowe pointed to the pony's feed tub. "He didn't finish his grain," he said. "Do you suppose something's wrong? I never knew a horse not to finish his grain."

"Certainly not Dime," Carole agreed. She went back to the office and told Mrs. Reg. Since horses can't talk, they can never tell anyone when they're sick. Carole knew to always watch for clues about their health. A sudden lack of appetite could be a sign of illness, particularly a digestive illness like colic; and colic could be very serious.

Maybe that's why Dime's been so horrid lately, Carole thought. *He isn't feeling well.* She felt a sudden rush of sympathy for the pony.

Mrs. Reg shook her head with concern when she heard the news. "I'll take his temperature and check his gut sounds," she said to Carole. "But Red told me he didn't eat all his food yesterday, either, and we couldn't find any other symptoms of illness."

"But he's been so strange lately," Carole said. "Maybe—"

"We'll keep a close eye on him," Mrs. Reg said. "Probably he just hasn't gotten enough exercise this winter. Don't worry, Carole. Whatever it is, we'll take care of it. He'll be feeling fine soon."

"I hope so," Carole said. "And Mrs. Reg? Mr. Stowe's working really hard." She didn't want Mrs. Reg to get too annoyed with him. He really was a nice old man.

To Carole's surprise, Mrs. Reg made an irritated face. "Yes, he seems very interested in working, doesn't he?" she said.

Now, what, wondered Carole, *is the matter with that?*

6

"So, Carole, I'm glad you didn't tell Mrs. Reg that we weren't riding today," Stevie said, a touch sarcastically, as she went into Belle's stall. It was Tuesday afternoon. Stevie's horse had apparently lain down in her stall overnight, because her back was covered with manure stains and pieces of sawdust bedding. Stevie sighed as she began to brush it off.

Carole ran her hand affectionately down Starlight's nose. "No, I wouldn't give up a riding lesson, not even for Mrs. Reg!" She thought for a moment, then corrected herself. "Well, I would, but only if she asked me. I wouldn't volunteer."

"I haven't seen Mr. Stowe today," Lisa said. "Maybe it will be a nice, normal day."

Just then someone screamed. It was a long, sad scream, more of a wail really, and it came from the indoor arena. The Saddle Club dropped their brushes and ran to investigate. They got to the gate of the arena just in time to see Dime careening past, riderless, with a wild look in his eye. The stirrups of his empty saddle banged against his sides as he ran.

"Oh, no," moaned Lisa. "Not again."

"Who fell off?" Stevie asked.

"One of the little kids," Carole realized. "Look. It's Jessica." On Tuesday afternoons Max taught a group of younger riders before he taught the lesson that The Saddle Club took. Inside the arena, five little kids were carefully holding their horses or ponies at a halt while Dime galloped in circles around them. In the center of the arena, Jessica was sitting on one of the fences, sobbing, while Max tried to console her.

Carole opened the gate. "Max, is she hurt?" she called. "Shall I get Mrs. Reg to call an ambulance?" They'd never had a serious accident at Pine Hollow, but Carole knew it could happen.

Max shook his head. "She's okay, she's just up-set," he said. "Could you three catch that pony before he spooks someone else's horse?"

"Dime bucked Jessica off twice," Liam informed them. "He bucked her off, and she got back on, and he bucked her off *again*."

It's no wonder she's crying, Lisa thought. Falling off was always embarrassing and sometimes scary; poor Jessica had to be completely demoralized. Lisa walked toward Dime quietly, making sooth-ing noises. Carole and Stevie did the same thing. Dime didn't want to be caught, but with three people after him he didn't have much choice. As soon as Carole grabbed his reins, he gave up the fight and stood quietly. Lisa and Stevie ran the stirrups up on both sides of the saddle; then they led Dime back to Jessica.

"Okay," Jessica said, gulping back tears. "I'll try again."

Max put his arm around her shoulder. "I'm proud of you for saying that, and I think you're a very good rider," he said. "I also think Dime is not going to behave today, and I don't think you're going to be able to have a good lesson with him. It's not your fault. I'd like you to get a differ-ent pony for the rest of the lesson."

Jessica looked relieved. "Okay, Max. But I would ride Dime."

"I know you would, I just don't think you should have to." Max looked up at The Saddle Club. "Could you guys take Dime in and get Peso for Jessica? That way she could catch her breath for a few more minutes."

"Of course," Stevie said instantly. "Carole, you take Dime in. Lisa and I will get Peso."

"I'll get his tack and meet you by his stall," Lisa said, hurrying into the stable. Stevie went to Peso's stall and started grooming him quickly. They didn't want Jessica to have to miss too much of her lesson.

Carole didn't need to hurry the way Stevie and Lisa did, and she was increasingly worried about Dime. What could spark such a huge behavioral change? In all the years Carole had ridden at Pine Hollow, she'd never known Dime to throw anyone deliberately, and here he'd done it three times in one week. Something had to be wrong.

Carole replaced Dime's bridle with his halter and fastened him to the cross-ties in the stable aisle. She was certain Dime couldn't be lame, because he'd looked perfectly sound every time he'd been galloping riderless in the last week. If his feet or legs were hurting, he would limp.

He could, however, be hurting somewhere else, and the most likely place seemed to Carole to be his back, because he kept bucking. She took his saddle off and carefully examined both it and Dime's girth for anything that could hurt him— any worn or broken places, any sharp edges, anything at all. Everything looked normal. Next she removed his saddle pad and went over it even more carefully. It was possible for a burr or a splinter or even a sharp piece of hay to get lodged in the pad. The saddle pad looked freshly laundered, and again, she couldn't find a thing.

Next Carole examined Dime's back, where the saddle rested, and his girthline, where the girth fastened around his middle. She looked for sores, scratches, bumps, clods of dirt, and anything else that might cause him discomfort when he was wearing a saddle. Nothing. Dime was well groomed and his skin was smooth.

Carole put her hands on Dime's back and pressed down. Could Dime have a pulled muscle? She couldn't find a single spot where he flinched or seemed to feel any pain.

"Dime," she said to him, "this would be so much easier if you could talk. What's the problem?"

Dime cocked one ear forward. He looked a little sulky, but other than that he seemed okay. He didn't have a runny nose or runny eyes, and he didn't cough.

Carole went to the tack room and came back with Max's stethoscope and horse thermometer. Even though Max always called the vet, Judy Barker, when one of the horses was sick, he kept these instruments on hand to help determine whether he should call her. Every responsible horse owner knew how to take a horse's vital signs. They were often the best clue to the horse's health.

Dime's temperature was 100 degrees, perfectly normal. Carole used the stethoscope to listen to his heartbeat and count his pulse. Those were normal, too.

"Just like Mrs. Reg said," Carole told him. "We can't find anything wrong with you." She counted the number of times Dime breathed in a minute, because if he was panting he could be in pain, but that, too, was normal. Finally she used the stethoscope to listen to Dime's gut.

Bra-AAP! The loud rumble made Carole giggle. She was always amused by how loudly horses' stomachs grumbled when heard through a stethoscope.

"You don't have colic," she informed the pony. When a horse colicked, its entire digestive system shut down, and its stomach and intestines made no noises. "I just don't know what's wrong with you. Dime, you've got to start behaving again."

Carole tried a little pep talk. "You're such a good pony. I know you can do it." While she brushed the sweat marks off Dime's back and the arena sand off his legs, she told him what a good pony he had always been, and how happy he had made the little boys and girls he helped teach to ride. She told him how valuable he was to Pine Hollow.

"We need nice ponies like you," she said as she unclipped the cross-ties and led Dime into his stall. "Look here, look out the window," she told him. "You can see the riding ring. Isn't your new stall nice? Max gave it to you because he wants you to be happy."

Dime turned and bared his teeth at her. Carole jerked her hand out of his way, and he sank his teeth into the sleeve of her coat. "Dime! Stop that!"

Lisa and Stevie came back up the aisle toward their horses. "Peso rolled in the pasture this morning, and it took ages for us to get him ready. We hurried as fast as we could." Stevie went back to Belle's stall and gave the mare a hug. "We'll have to hurry now to get ready for our own lesson."

Lisa saw the strange expression on Carole's face. "What's wrong?" she asked.

"Dime just tried to bite me," Carole said in amazement. "He seemed okay, and I was telling him what a good pony he is, and how much Max depends on him, and when I put him back in his stall he tried to bite me."

Lisa looked into the pony's stall. "He hasn't finished his grain today, either."

Carole sighed. "I guess I'd better tell Mrs. Reg. Something has to be wrong with him."

Stevie shook her head. "I wish we knew what it was. I don't think he's going to shape up until we fix whatever it is. Do you think his back hurts, Carole?"

Carole shook her head. "I checked, as well as I could."

Lisa looked again at the grain bucket. "And he's not colicking?"

"I don't see how he can be," Carole said in exasperation. "His stomach is rumbling like a freight train!"

"Well, it must be something," Stevie said with a sigh.

Carole bit her lip anxiously. She was starting to really worry about the little pony.

LISA DIDN'T HAVE the best lesson of her entire life, but she enjoyed the chance to ride Prancer again. Much as she loved trail rides, she also loved lessons, because they gave her the chance to improve specific skills. Of course, on the trail she had plenty of opportunities to improve her general riding and horse handling, but there she rarely thought about the finer points of body control; for example, whether her heels were down as much as they could be or whether Prancer's neck was curving gently through the turns.

Today Max had them riding over fences without their stirrups. This was something Lisa would never practice on the trail, because she found it a little nerve-racking, but she had to admit it was great for her leg position. Without stirrups, it was easy to let your leg swing loose, but over a jump you didn't dare!

Lisa knew, too, that her confidence had been shaken by that horrible Pony Club rally. After an hour of jumping she felt proud of herself and of Prancer, and her confidence was restored. Stevie and Carole also rode well, so Lisa was sure they would both feel better, too.

"Wasn't that great!" Carole said as they began walking their horses up and down the driveway to cool them off before they untacked them. "Starlight just flew, and riding without stirrups is so much fun!"

Lisa wouldn't have called it fun. She laughed at her friend's enthusiasm. Carole truly loved everything about horses.

"Stevie, Belle looked fantastic!" Carole continued. "Remember last week when she didn't want to jump the brush box? She never even looked at it today—she just went over it!"

"Yeah." Stevie reached up to stroke Belle's neck, but she didn't sound as happy as either of her friends thought she should. "It was a good lesson, but you know, I just can't stop thinking about Mrs. Reg and her total lack of imagination regarding the dance. Balloons and streamers! Everyone does balloons and streamers!

"It's just so mundane," Stevie continued. "And that's not all. Phil told me they're hiring a DJ for his school dance. I asked Mrs. Reg if we could hire a DJ, since she insists that we can't have a live band, and she said it was too expensive!"

"It probably is too expensive," Lisa said. "Phil's school probably charges an admission fee for the dance, and, anyway, the school would have a budget for social activities. This barn dance is just something Max and Mrs. Reg do because they're nice. It's just so we can all have fun."

Lisa exchanged looks with Carole. They were thinking the same thing, that Stevie was making way too big a deal over the dance. She only saw Phil every few weeks anyway. Why was Valentine's Day such a big deal? And if it *was* such a big deal, why didn't Stevie just go to Phil's dance?

Lisa wondered if she would understand better if she had her own boyfriend.

"How can it be too expensive when it's so important?" Stevie demanded.

"How can what be too expensive?" a friendly voice asked.

The three girls turned. "Mr. Stowe!" said Lisa. "What a surprise!"

"The horses don't need to rest today, do they?" he asked with the glint of a smile in his eye.

"No . . . ," said Carole. She wondered what job she could find to keep Mr. Stowe out of Mrs. Reg's hair today. Red usually cleaned the stalls early in the mornings on weekdays.

"What is too expensive and so important?" Mr. Stowe asked Stevie again.

"The Valentine's Day dance!" she exploded. "We want it to be special, and the decorations are very important."

"I don't think Phil is going to change his mind and come to Pine Hollow if our decorations are better than his," Lisa said quietly. She didn't want to upset Stevie, but she did think she was pinning too much hope on a bunch of balloons.

Stevie looked angry. "Atmosphere is extremely important. Every last detail counts. You know Mrs. Reg always says that."

"But she wasn't talking about a dance—" Lisa began. Carole elbowed her in the ribs, and Lisa shut her mouth. She understood what Carole meant, that anything Lisa said was only going to

76

annoy Stevie more. Stevie wasn't being logical, but they had never been able to make her be logical. The best they could do was be her friend.

Lisa remembered when Mrs. Reg had given a talk about atmosphere and details. She'd been talking about stable management during a Pony Club rally! She meant all the bridles had to be on hooks, and the water buckets in the stalls tied at the proper heights, and things like that. She hadn't been talking about DJs or paper streamers.

"Mrs. Reg is in charge of the decorations for the dance, but she's been so busy and *distracted* lately that she's just not able to give them much time," Stevie told Mr. Stowe sadly. "Of course, I want the barn to look nice because I expect that my boyfriend, Phil, will be coming. But that's not the only reason. The reputation of Pine Hollow is at stake."

Carole made a choking noise.

"Elizabeth wants the place to look nice, but she doesn't want to spend a lot of money, is that it?" Mr. Stowe asked.

"That's it exactly," said Stevie. "I think Max must have put her on a very tight budget." She sighed dramatically. "If this barn dance isn't absolutely spectacular, I think my love life will be over."

Mr. Stowe looked concerned. "We can't let that happen," he said.

Lisa and Carole looked at one another in amazement. Could they have heard Mr. Stowe right? Could he be concerned about Stevie's love life? Carole thought Stevie was laying it on just a bit too thick. If her love life ended this Valentine's Day, it would be because she and Phil were both so stubborn, not because the hay barn wasn't pretty enough.

"Seriously?" Stevie asked. Even she sounded surprised.

"Seriously," Mr. Stowe said. "I'm more than happy to be of assistance to Elizabeth."

"Eli—oh, right." None of The Saddle Club had gotten used to Mrs. Reg's being called Elizabeth.

Carole ran her hand down Starlight's chest. It no longer felt warm or sweaty. "Let's take them inside," she suggested. The wind had picked up, and she was starting to feel cold.

Mr. Stowe followed them down the stable aisle. "What did you all have in mind?"

"Not much," Lisa said. "Stevie's the mastermind."

Stevie smiled modestly. "I'm not suggesting anything out of the ordinary," she said. "I realize a laser light show is probably too expensive, and I guess all the best local bands are probably booked by now. But I do think we should get a DJ instead of using Max's CDs."

"What's wrong with his CDs?" Mr. Stowe said. "Doesn't he have good ones?"

Stevie shrugged. "They're fine. It's just a DJ is—you know—most dances have a DJ, to change the CDs and introduce the songs."

Mr. Stowe shook his head. "For a Valentine's Day dance you want pure romance," he said.

"Totally," said Stevie.

"So you don't want some wisecracking high-school kid interrupting the music every couple of minutes," he continued. "Where's the atmosphere in that? What we need to do is find an automatic

CD changer and cue up a bunch of music so that it just flows, one romantic love song into another."

Stevie blinked. "That'd be perfect," she said. She could imagine herself dancing with Phil, flowing from one song to another.

"There's nothing wrong with balloons or streamers," Mr. Stowe continued, "but for atmosphere you need to control the lighting."

"Max has a few strings of regular lightbulbs," Lisa said. "We usually use those."

"But they're bright, right?" he asked. Carole nodded. "So what if you get some of those little paper lanterns to cover all the bulbs," Mr. Stowe suggested. "And if you got low-wattage bulbs in the first place, you could have a nice, soft, romantic light. And then—I've got the perfect idea! But it's a surprise. I won't even tell you girls." He smiled. "The perfect surprise for a romantic barn dance."

"What about a strobe light?" Stevie said. "I was really hoping for a strobe light."

"A strobe light!" Mr. Stowe shook his head. "That's one of those things that makes everyone look like they're jerking when they dance, isn't it?"

"It's kind of fun," Carole said. "People look like they stop and then start again."

"But is it *romantic?*" Mr. Stowe asked, with a sweep of his hands.

"No," said Carole. "I guess not."

"The name of this game has to be romance," he said. "It's a romantic time of year; we have to create and nourish the proper atmosphere. No strobes. No mouthy DJs. Nothing but pure romance."

Lisa drew in a breath. For a moment Mr. Stowe was utterly transformed. Lisa had seen actors on stage turn instantly from one character into another, but she had never seen it happen in life before. Suddenly Mr. Stowe seemed younger, more dapper, almost charming. Lisa was dazzled.

"Max!" Mrs. Reg shouted down the aisle. "Did you remember to buy that worm paste?"

Mr. Stowe jumped and suddenly looked sheepish. The dapper gentleman vanished, and in his place was old, kind, helpful Mr. Stowe.

Carole settled Starlight in his stall and gave him a good-bye pat. She, too, had seen something special in Mr. Stowe a moment ago. He had seemed like a man of vision and ideas, instead of a man learning how to ride. She turned to him with friendly pity. "I'm going to check Dime's pulse again," she said. "Would you like me to show you how?"

Mr. Stowe half shrugged. "That's kind of you, but I wouldn't want to trouble you," he said.

"It's no trouble," Carole said. She went for the stethoscope.

"No, really . . . ," Mr. Stowe called to her retreating back. He shrugged again to Lisa and Stevie. "You girls don't need to take so much trouble with me," he said.

"It's no trouble at all," Stevie said sincerely. She was so pleased with Mr. Stowe's ideas—paper lanterns would be much more romantic than a strobe light. Why hadn't she realized that? And to think that Phil was excited about his school's strobe light! He just didn't know what true romance was. "Besides, Carole really loves to teach people about horses."

"I can tell." Mr. Stowe sighed.

Mrs. Reg came down the aisle toward them. "Hello, Howard. I see you found these girls again," she said, a bit sharply. "What horse project have they dragged you into this time?"

Mr. Stowe swept his hat off. He seemed a little confused by the tone of Mrs. Reg's voice. "Good afternoon, Elizabeth," he said politely.

"He's very interested in horses, Mrs. Reg," Stevie said, rushing to his defense. How could Mrs. Reg be rude to him? Suddenly Stevie wanted Mr. Stowe to keep coming to Pine Hollow so that he could help them with the dance. He was saving her chance with Phil! "He's learned a lot in the last week."

"I see." Mrs. Reg sounded oddly skeptical.

To Stevie's and Lisa's surprise, Mr. Stowe blushed. "I've found a lot around Pine Hollow to be interested in," he said softly. Mrs. Reg gave him another slightly disgruntled look and walked away.

"Why, Mr. Stowe," Carole said, coming back from the tack room with the stethoscope in her hands, "what's wrong?"

"Mrs. Reg is in a bad mood," Stevie said hotly.

"Don't worry about her," Carole said gently. "She never minds it when we hang around the stable, as long as we're doing something useful. Now, here's the stable stethoscope. Let's go see Dime."

"I guess I might as well," Mr. Stowe said. He

followed them down the aisle. Carole led the way, worried about Dime. Stevie walked after her, worried about Phil. Lisa trailed Stevie. She was worried about Mrs. Reg and why the sad look was back in her eyes.

LISA LEANED BACK against the pillows she'd thrown on the floor of her bedroom. "What a week," she said. "I'm glad it's Friday."

"Me too," agreed Carole, reaching for a handful of popcorn from the bowl sitting next to Lisa. The Saddle Club was staying at Lisa's house the whole weekend. "I feel like we haven't solved any of the problems we've had this week!"

"Problems?" asked Stevie, pulling the popcorn bowl a little closer to her side. "You mean *problem*. Phil—"

"Don't forget Dime," Carole said quickly. She didn't want to get Stevie started on the subject of Phil, and as far as Carole was concerned, Dime was the biggest problem of the week. The little pony was still miserable and cranky, and now it was obvious that he had started to lose weight. Something was clearly wrong, but no one knew what.

"Poor Dime," Lisa said softly. "Max called the vet about him this afternoon."

"His vital signs are still all normal, though," Carole said. "I just don't know what it could be." Her face clouded with worry.

"Judy'll figure it out," Stevie said comfortingly. She was awfully upset about Phil, but she had enough worry left over to spend on Dime. Still, Judy was a very good vet, and she had always been able to cure all the Pine Hollow horses so far, except for Pepper, who had had to be put to sleep because of extreme old age. "How old is Dime?" Stevie asked.

Lisa's eyes widened when she realized what Stevie was thinking. She had loved Pepper, and his death had been very hard on her.

"Not that old," Carole said, putting a comforting hand on Lisa's arm. "I think he's in his early twenties, but ponies live a long time, longer than horses, usually."

"Good," Lisa said. "We can't lose Dime."

"Of course not!" Carole said quickly. Up until that point she'd only worried about Dime being in pain from some unknown injury. She'd never thought of Dime's dying.

"Of course not," Stevie echoed. "He doesn't look that bad. But he'll have to shape up soon, or I don't know what Max will do with him. He hasn't been able to be used in lessons all week." The girls sighed. Dime's behavior hadn't improved at all. He'd even nipped Red.

"Penny's been a little out of sorts, too," Carole said. "I hope whatever Dime has isn't contagious."

Someone knocked on Lisa's bedroom door. It was Lisa's mother. "Look, dear!" she said, coming into the room. "I saw this at the store this evening, so I bought it for you to wear to your dance! Isn't it cute?" Mrs. Atwood worked part-time at a fashion shop in the Willow Creek Mall. She held up a fluffy angora tunic sweater with hearts embroidered down the sleeves. It was hot pink—very hot.

Lisa blinked. "Gee—I, uh—thanks, Mom!" she stammered. Lisa's mother enjoyed shopping much more than Lisa did, so it wasn't unusual for her to buy Lisa clothes on the spur of the moment. However, she usually bought preppy, conservative, little-girl things. This tunic was wild.

"Geez," Stevie said when Mrs. Atwood had gone. "You'll outshine Veronica! I think this is the same color as those breeches she was trying to impress Simon with."

"Maybe she'll loan me the breeches," Lisa said. "Then I can be the same color from head to toe." Her friends stared at her until they realized that she was joking.

"The same very bright color!" Carole said, starting to laugh.

Lisa pulled her sweatshirt off and tried the sweater on in front of her mirror. It reached nearly to her knees, but the sleeves and shoulders fit her well. It *was* very bright, but she kind of liked it.

"You'll attract attention," Stevie remarked. "People will think you're on fire."

Lisa stuck out her tongue, then went back to the mirror. "Should I really wear this? My mother might be disappointed if I don't—and I kind of like it—but I never wear stuff like this."

"Of course you'll wear it," Carole said firmly. "It's cool. Wear your black leggings instead of your blue jeans, put your black turtleneck on under the sweater, and tie your hair back with a black bow. That'll tone the color down a little, and you'll look fabulous."

Lisa smiled. "Good idea! I think I will wear it. I was going to wear my red sweater again, and my turtleneck with the hearts. What are you going to wear, Carole?"

Carole shrugged. "I haven't got anything with hearts on it. I thought I'd just wear the navy sweater Aunt Jessie sent me for Christmas."

"Why don't you wear my red one instead?"

Carole smiled. "That'd be great! Thank you. How about you, Stevie? What are you going to wear?"

Stevie scowled. "It's hardly going to matter. The person I most want to see me isn't going to be there."

Carole and Lisa looked at each other. Lisa changed back into her sweatshirt, neatly folded her new sweater, and sat down on the floor beside Stevie. Carole sat down on Stevie's other side.

"Haven't you and Phil gotten this worked out yet?" Lisa asked. She felt a little bad; she'd been avoiding the subject with Stevie, even though she knew her friend was upset. Lisa just wasn't sure she sympathized with her on this one—at least, not entirely. And it was hard to hear someone complain about her boyfriend when she didn't have one.

"We haven't worked anything out at all," Stevie said. "I've talked to him every night this week, but we never get anywhere except into another fight. We keep having one of those did-not did-too conversations, like I used to have with my brothers, only these are more like 'Mine!' 'No, mine!' We're not getting anywhere."

"I remember having an argument like that when I was really little," Carole said. "I was staying with my cousin, and we kept fighting over this funny windup toy. It got so bad that my mother finally went out and bought a duplicate so that we could each play with our own."

Stevie gave her a despairing look. "That's the situation we already have!" she said. "We've got two dances! What we need is only one!" She paused, then raised an eyebrow. "Maybe we could get Phil's school closed by the county board of health. That might work."

Lisa laughed, but she could tell that Stevie was just barely joking. If she got much more worked up, she might do something stupid. Lisa wouldn't put it past Stevie to empty her brother Michael's ant farm into Phil's school cafeteria, then call the county inspectors about an infestation.

"I know you're upset," she said gently, "but I think Phil has a point, too. He's spent a lot of time organizing this dance, and he's probably worked very hard. Of course he wants to show it off to you. You're the person whose opinion matters most to him!"

"My opinion is that he should come to *my* dance," Stevie retorted. "I understand what you're saying, Lisa, but I should be more important to him than any crummy dance, whether he's worked on the committee or not. If he really, truly cared about me, he would skip his dance. What's the point of Valentine's Day anyway, if you can't spend it with the person you care about?"

"Maybe you can do both dances," Carole suggested. "Spend half the night at Pine Hollow, and half the night at his school."

"We'd spend half the night in the car, going back and forth between dances," Stevie said impatiently. "Besides, I wouldn't get to hang around you guys very much. This isn't just about our dances anymore. This is an argument about a principle. Phil should come to Pine Hollow because it's important to me."

Carole and Lisa sighed. Carole didn't know what else to say. When Stevie went downstairs to get more sodas, Carole turned to Lisa. "You know, I bet Phil's sitting at home right now, thinking, 'Stevie should go to my school dance because it's important to me. If she truly cared about me, she would skip her dance.'"

Lisa chewed a piece of the ice left in her glass. "I know. You and I can both see that Phil's side of the story is just as good as—in fact, it's probably identical to—Stevie's, but Stevie can't see it at all. I'm not sure we can convince her, either."

Carole nodded. "Stevie really wants to get her own way on this. I don't think we can do anything, except hang around to console her when she breaks up with Phil."

Lisa shook her head. "Seems like a stupid reason to lose a boyfriend."

"I've got it!" Stevie threw open Lisa's door so hard that one of the open cans of sodas she was carrying spilled. The girls spent several minutes mopping Lisa's carpet with some bathroom towels.

"Sorry," Stevie said. "At least it was diet lemon-lime. No stickys, no stains. But I've come up with a really excellent plan!" She settled herself on the floor and took a long sip of one of the remaining sodas. "Tomorrow, after Horse Wise has finished helping Mrs. Reg decorate the hay barn, I'm going to invite Phil to come see it. When he sees how wonderfully, perfectly romantic it's going to be—how much nicer than that smelly, linoleum-covered cafeteria—I know he'll want to come to our dance."

Lisa wasn't convinced this scheme would work, but it was a lot less destructive than having Phil's school condemned. She gladly offered Stevie her phone to call Phil right away.

Stevie called and hung up grinning. "He said he was happy to come," she reported. "His mom's taking him into town anyway so that he can put the finishing touches on his cafeteria. He's coming at noon." She laughed. "Carole, Lisa, I feel so much better! This is going to be a great Valentine's Day after all!"

"WHAT A BEAUTIFUL morning," Carole said. She paused to sniff the springlike air before helping Lisa push the two heavy doors of Pine Hollow's hay barn open. At the end of summer, the hay barn was filled top to bottom and edge to edge with bales of hay for the Pine Hollow horses. By February, however, the supply of hay was always getting low enough that the main floor of the old-fashioned barn was completely clear. Now Horse Wise was setting up for the evening's festivities. Adam, Polly, and a few of the other Pony Clubbers climbed into the loft and threw some hay bales down. The rest of the kids stacked them at the sides of the barn to make seats and tables for the dance.

"Just angle those bales a little more to the left, Betsy," Stevie directed. "We want to create a cozy atmosphere."

"Who died and made you director of operations?" Betsy asked. She pushed her bales flat against the wall.

"It's a much cozier atmosphere," Stevie said cheerily, adjusting Betsy's bales for her. Betsy walked away without saying anything.

"Don't let Betsy bug you," Meg whispered to Stevie and Lisa. "Adam hasn't asked her to the dance yet, and she's a little upset."

Stevie patted Meg's arm conspiratorially. "When we got here I saw something red fall out of Adam's pocket. He picked it back up, but it looked like a heart. Like an invitation. Tell Betsy not to worry."

Meg brightened. "Thanks."

Stevie waved her hand. "Don't mention it." To Lisa she added, "Love is in the air today. Love is everywhere today."

"Don't mention it," Lisa said. Since the moment Stevie had talked to Phil the night before, she'd been awash with romance. Lisa was afraid she and Carole would drown in Stevie's sentiment before the night was over.

When the hay bales were set up to Stevie's satisfaction, the younger kids swept the loose hay from the floor. The Saddle Club brought out the string of lights and showed everyone how to hang the paper lanterns over the bare bulbs. Max brought in his CD player and speakers, and Lisa helped him set the automatic changer he'd borrowed so that the first hour's worth of music would play continuously.

"Make the first song 'Just As Long As We're Together,'" Stevie said, coming over from where she was telling Simon and Polly exactly how to hang the lights. "It's our song—Phil's and mine."

This was news to Lisa, but she put the song on

first anyway. *At least one member of The Saddle Club is going to have a perfect evening*, she thought.

"Here, Veronica," said Stevie, "why don't you blow up these balloons? You've got plenty of hot air."

Veronica took the balloons from Stevie without comment. "Simon? Oh, Simon? Could you help me with these balloons?" Simon came down from the ladder and walked across the room to her. Lisa couldn't help noticing how cool his walk was. Simon had been such a geek. How could anyone change so much in such a short time?

"Sure," he said to Veronica.

"Oh, thanks. It takes such strong lungs to blow up balloons."

"Oh, barf," Lisa whispered to Stevie.

"You are coming to the dance tonight, aren't you?" Veronica continued.

"Of course," Simon said. "I wouldn't miss it."

"I didn't think so," Veronica said sweetly.

Lisa smiled to herself. So Simon hadn't asked Veronica! Maybe she and Carole wouldn't be the only people their age without dates for the dance.

Carole was hanging white and pink twisted streamers near the door when she saw Mr. Stowe pull up outside. She waved to him. He came to the door and looked inside, rubbing his hands together happily. "This looks great," he said. "Don't worry, I brought my surprise. But I'm not telling you yet—it might get back to Elizabeth. You kids let me know when you're all the way done."

"Okay," Carole said, amused by his interest. Not too many old men would be so interested in a young persons' dance.

THEY HAD JUST finished when Phil's mother pulled up and Phil hopped out of the car. Stevie rushed out to greet him.

"We'll go check on Dime," Carole said, pulling Lisa along with her.

"Thanks," Stevie called back gratefully. She wanted this special moment alone with Phil—this special moment when he told her how important she was to him.

"Look," she said as they walked into the barn holding hands, "isn't this romantic?" She showed him the lights and the balloons and the streamers. She told him which song would play first on the stereo. She pointed out the hay bales artfully arranged in the corners.

Phil seemed interested in everything. "It really

looks super," he said. "You guys have done a great job. I wish we'd thought of the paper lanterns."

They stood in the middle of the floor, holding hands and smiling at one another.

"It'll be perfectly romantic," said Stevie.

Phil looked at her expectantly. "Now are you going to tell me?" he asked.

Stevie frowned. "Tell you what?"

"That you're coming to my dance. That's why you wanted me here this afternoon, isn't it? Because I wouldn't be able to see the barn otherwise. Thanks, Stevie. It's a great surprise."

Stevie couldn't believe her ears. "The surprise is what a jerk you are!" she said. "This was supposed to make you want to come to my dance!"

Phil's expression changed to fury. "Well, I don't!" he said. "I want to go to my dance!"

"Then go!" Stevie shouted. "I'm not going with you! I hope you have a great time dancing with all the other girls!"

"Fine!" Phil turned on his heel and went back to his mother's car. He slammed the door.

"Fine!" Stevie shouted after him, but she'd never felt worse in her life.

CAROLE FITTED THE earpieces of Max's stethoscope into her ears and set the end of it gently against Dime's belly. "Listen," she said, taking the earpieces out and handing them to Lisa. "He really does sound rumbly. It can't be colic."

"But he's still not eating," Lisa said sadly. She patted Dime's flank, and the pony gave her an angry look, his ears pinned against his head. Carole held Dime's lead rope firmly.

"Feel his ribs," Carole said. "They're starting to stick out. He's losing weight. Poor pony. Red made him a bran mash today, and he didn't even eat all of that."

"I asked Max what Judy said," Lisa reported.

"He said she couldn't find anything wrong either, but she drew some blood to send away for tests. She'll get the results back in a few days."

Carole nodded. "Good. That'll tell us if there's any infection or—"

"I hate him!" Stevie flew into the stall, howling with sadness and rage. She threw her arms around Dime and sobbed into the pony's mane. "He is such a jerk! I hate him!" she cried between sobs.

"Oh no," Carole said. "What happened?"

"He's going to his dance with someone else!" Stevie sobbed harder. Dime, for a change, seemed sympathetic—he turned and nuzzled Stevie's shoulder. Carole and Lisa looked at each other in shocked silence.

"With someone else?" Lisa asked.

"How could he?" said Carole. "That's horrid!"

"I just hate him," Stevie replied. "He's such a jerk. It's over between us, entirely over."

Lisa patted her on the back. "I can't believe it," she said indignantly. "Who's he going with?"

"Oh, I don't know." Stevie wiped her eyes on the back of her sleeve and smoothed Dime's rumpled mane. "He thought—he actually thought that I asked him to come see the hay barn because I was going to his dance. He said he didn't want to come here, and I said I didn't want to go there and that I hoped he had fun dancing with all the other girls, and I know he will and I hate him, I really do." She hiccuped back another sob.

"So he didn't actually ask anyone else to his dance?" Carole said.

"Well, no, of course not! But he'll probably meet someone else there he likes better—I mean, it's obvious he doesn't care about me."

"Oh, Stevie." Carole slumped against the wall of the stall. Dime pinned his ears back at her, and Lisa grabbed his lead rope and spoke sharply to him. She couldn't believe Stevie had made such a mess over what really was a little dance. Well, no, she could believe it—Stevie sometimes made big messes over small things. Lisa tried to imagine whether she would get this worked up if John Brightstar, her friend out West, had done something similar. She didn't think so. She seldom got as upset over anything as Stevie did. Lisa sighed. She wished she could go to a Valentine's Day dance with John. She'd go to his school. She wouldn't care. Too bad he was two thousand miles away.

Carole had seen Dime put his ears back again, and even though she was concerned for Stevie, that bothered her more. Why was this usually cheerful pony acting so ugly? Carole didn't know what else to do for him. She knew Max was already doing everything he could.

Stevie sat down next to Carole and buried her head in her arms. "I thought it was going to be such a nice evening," she said. "I was really hoping for a nice time." Carole shook her head sadly. All along she'd thought Stevie was overreacting, but now the misery in Stevie's voice hurt her heart. Why couldn't Stevie and Phil have worked it out? They were both going to be unhappy now.

"Well," Lisa said after a long, depressing pause, "I suppose we should go ride."

"I suppose so," Carole said. "Starlight needs the exercise. Stevie?"

Stevie rose to her feet. "Yeah. I mean, that's what we planned to do. We might as well do it." She couldn't remember when she'd been less enthusiastic about a trail ride. For a moment she thought of all the special rides she'd taken with Phil, but that only made her feel worse. They had had a lot of fun together, but it was over now.

The girls gathered their grooming equipment and tack and began to prepare their horses. Standing in Starlight's stall brushing the dust from his glossy flanks, Carole began to feel just a little bit better. Anyone who owned a horse like Starlight couldn't feel depressed for long. She leaned against him.

"Hey! My favorite young ladies! Would you by any chance be going on another trail ride?" Mr. Stowe came around the corner of the aisle, a saddle in his arms, smiling broadly.

Stevie smiled listlessly in return. "Good guess," she said.

"Hello, Mr. Stowe," Carole said. "Did you finish your surprise?"

Mr. Stowe made hushing movements with his hands. "Not yet," he said. "No, I thought I'd go for a ride with you girls first. That is, if you don't mind."

Stevie rolled her eyes at Lisa in dismay. Lisa understood, but what could they say? Mr. Stowe had been so nice to them.

"Sure," Carole said faintly. It was the only polite answer.

Mr. Stowe secured Delilah on a set of cross-ties just outside Starlight's stall and began grooming her. "I've got my secret hidden in my car," he whispered to Carole over the door of Starlight's stall. "Elizabeth's car is still in for repair, and she was just asking me for another ride. I can't have her see the secret! So I told her I was going to ride with you right now." He moved to Delilah's other side, and as a consequence he spoke more loudly. "I'd like to stay away from Elizabeth for a little while."

Carole looked up from combing Starlight's tail. She saw Mrs. Reg come around the corner and then stop, facing Mr. Stowe's back. Mrs. Reg's smile faded away, and a hurt expression took its place. She looked at Mr. Stowe's back for another moment, then turned on her heel and left.

Carole stood still for a moment, puzzled and too surprised to say anything. Why did Mrs. Reg look so upset? All Mr. Stowe had said was that he'd like to stay away from her. Carole turned this phrase over in her mind, trying to decide whether it would upset her. It probably wouldn't be the nicest thing to hear, she decided, but it wouldn't be that bad. But Mrs. Reg had looked really hurt—stunned and disappointed.

Carole didn't say anything to the other girls, because she didn't want Mr. Stowe to know that he'd upset Mrs. Reg. He hadn't done it on purpose, after all. But she continued to wonder about it even after they were mounted and riding through the bare trails.

Mr. Stowe seemed conscious of how morose they all were. *How could he not be,* Carole thought, *when none of us is laughing or even talking?*

"I do hope you all would have told me if you didn't want an old man's company," he said. "I wouldn't have been offended, honest now."

"We would have told you," Lisa assured him. What difference did it make if Mr. Stowe went with them? "We're just a little worried—about one of the ponies, and about the dance."

"The dance'll be fine. You three'll be sur-rounded by beaus."

"Bows?" asked Stevie. "The only one of us who wears ribbons is Lisa."

Mr. Stowe laughed heartily, as though Stevie had made a joke. Stevie sighed. She couldn't make a joke right now if she tried.

"Oh, my gosh," Carole said softly.

"What's wrong?" Lisa drew Prancer to a walk.

"Nothing," Carole said with a quick shake of her head. But it *was* something. She suddenly un-derstood why Mrs. Reg looked so upset. Mrs. Reg liked Mr. Stowe. *Liked* him liked him! Like as a boyfriend!

Poor Mrs. Reg. Carole looked at gangly Mr. Stowe, who was slap-trotting alongside her, and felt more depressed than ever.

"Hey, Stevie," Mr. Stowe said, "here's one for you. How many dummies does it take to screw in a lightbulb?"

"How many?" Stevie asked dully.

"Six," he said. "One to hold the lightbulb, and five to turn the ladder around."

Stevie and Lisa laughed, but Carole didn't even try. She felt so sorry for Mrs. Reg. Then she felt sorry for them all. It was Valentine's Day, and Pine Hollow was full of broken hearts.

WHEN THEY GOT back to Pine Hollow, they saw Mrs. Reg in the outdoor arena, schooling Eve, a beautiful gray mare Max had adopted not long ago. Eve had been rescued from an abusive owner and was just starting to recover her trust in people. Mrs. Reg had taken her on as a special project. The mare was beginning to flourish.

"Look at that!" Stevie said, bringing Belle to a halt outside the ring. "Mrs. Reg is riding Eve!" Mrs. Reg trotted a circle, and Eve delicately mouthed the bit.

Carole beamed. "They're starting to really work together. Look—you can see how much Eve is cooperating."

Lisa felt too proud and happy to speak. After such a depressing afternoon, seeing Eve go so well under saddle was like a special gift. When Eve had first been rescued, Lisa had worked harder than any of the rest of them to help her find the courage to live.

Mr. Stowe, too, was silent for a moment, watching Mrs. Reg ride the gray mare. Mrs. Reg, thought Carole, looked truly beautiful on a horse. She rode as gracefully as a young girl, and there was something about her growing relationship with Eve that was wonderful to see. Carole fought a sudden urge to tell Mr. Stowe what she suspected of Mrs. Reg's feelings.

"Yep, that's a pretty little filly, all right," Mr. Stowe said. "I always did like them Thoroughbreds."

"Eve's not a Thoroughbred," Carole said, turning away from him with a slight feeling of annoyance. Poor Mrs. Reg!

Mr. Stowe dismounted and loosened Delilah's girth. "After I get this horse put away, I'm going to go set up my surprise," he said. "I want you all to promise me, no peeking until the dance starts. And no telling Elizabeth, either."

"We promise." Stevie buried her face in Belle's

neck as she had in Dime's. She didn't care about Mr. Stowe's surprise anymore, and she doubted Lisa and Carole were very excited, either. The knot she'd had in her stomach ever since Phil drove away would not unravel. The only reason she was going to the dance at all was because it would beat staying home with her bratty brothers.

Carole waited until Mr. Stowe had put Delilah away and left the main stable before telling her friends what she thought.

"No way!" Stevie said. "Mrs. Reg likes Mr. Stowe? That's unbelievable."

"It is," Lisa agreed. She pulled Prancer's bridle off and scratched the mare behind the ears. "I'm sorry, Carole, but it doesn't make sense. It doesn't sound possible."

"Why not?" Carole asked bluntly.

"I mean—we're talking about Mrs. Reg!" Stevie sputtered. "She can't feel like that for anyone! She was married, for one thing. To Max the Second."

"Max the Second has been dead for an awfully long time," Lisa argued. "I bet Mrs. Reg probably would like to have someone to go to movies with, and out to dinner and stuff like that. She probably would like a boyfriend. I just can't imagine her going out with Mr. Stowe."

"I would agree with you guys except that I saw her face," Carole persisted. "She wouldn't look that upset for any other reason. I'm sure I'm right. She likes Mr. Stowe." She put Starlight back in his stall. Lisa and Stevie put Prancer and Belle away, too, and they met in the center of the aisle.

"It's too bad Mr. Stowe doesn't like her back," Lisa said at last.

"I know," Carole replied. "I couldn't believe he didn't say anything about how nice she looked out there on Eve. I think he only saw the horse. I don't think he noticed Mrs. Reg at all."

"Men," Stevie said heavily. "They're all creeps. Still, maybe we could do something about Mrs. Reg and Mr. Stowe. Maybe we could—"

"No." Carole cut in firmly. "We can't do anything about this at all."

"I agree," Lisa said. "All we'd probably end up doing is embarrassing Mrs. Reg, and I'd never risk that." She checked her watch. "Come on. Let's go back to my house. It's time to get ready for the dance."

They put their gear away, put on their winter

jackets, and started walking to Lisa's house. "Imagine someone liking Mr. Stowe!" Stevie said, shaking her head.

"I know," said Carole, sighing. "He's so old."

"WHAT ARE YOU wearing, Stevie?" Lisa asked. She modeled her new sweater in front of her mirror. Carole's suggestions had been good. The sweater looked great over black leggings and a black turtleneck.

"I don't know," Stevie said. "What difference does it make now?"

"You must have brought something to wear," Carole said. "What were you planning on wearing when you thought Phil was coming?" She pulled Lisa's red sweater over her head.

"That's just it," Stevie said with a sigh. "I couldn't think of anything I liked well enough. I've outgrown some of my favorite stuff. And now I just don't care. I'm so angry at Phil. The creep."

"So you came to spend two nights at my house, and you didn't bring anything to wear to the dance?" Lisa asked.

"Well . . ." Stevie looked vaguely embarrassed. "I meant to ask you guys for help last night, but I got so excited after I talked to Phil

112

that I forgot. It doesn't really matter. I'll just wear what I have on."

Lisa looked at Stevie's torn, dirty jeans, old gray sweatshirt, and cream-colored turtleneck. She went into her closet and started rummaging around. "Here are some clean jeans," she said, tossing Stevie a pair. "And here. How about this?" She held up a dainty white sweater with pearl buttons and a lace collar.

"Uh, Lisa, no offense—"

Carole cut in. "It's not exactly Stevie's style."

Lisa looked at the sweater again. "Guess not. No. It's not even really my style, but it looks sort of valentiney."

"I don't feel valentiney," Stevie declared.

"That's the problem," Carole said. "None of us does. Stevie, I have an idea. You wear the sweater I was going to wear—the one Aunt Jessie gave me. It's navy, so it'll go with your turtleneck."

"It'll go with my mood, too," said Stevie. "I feel blue. It's just not *right* to be separated from your boyfriend on Valentine's Day." She buttoned the clean jeans. "Thanks for the clothes, though."

Lisa felt a twinge of exasperation. "You know, Stevie, you don't have to be separated from Phil," she said.

Carole twisted her ponytail and pinned it against her head. "Poor Dime," she said whimsically. "Maybe that's his problem. Do you suppose he has a girlfriend that he doesn't want to be apart from?"

Lisa turned around and stared at Carole. "That's it!" she said.

"WHAT'S IT?" Carole asked.

"The problem with Dime! You've solved it!" Lisa was so excited that she grabbed Carole's hands and started swinging her around the room.

"How did I solve it?" Carole looked confused. "All I said was do you think he has a girlfriend. I was *joking*."

"But what if he does have one? What if it's Penny? It *is* Penny—that makes perfect sense!" Lisa sat down and started pulling on her paddock boots. "Come on, hurry! We've got to get to Pine Hollow."

Stevie sat down beside Lisa and slowly pulled on her cowboy boots. Carole remained standing, her hands on her hips and a perplexed look on her face. "You really think that's it?" she asked. "I mean, I know horses form friendships—"

"And you know that sometimes those friendships can be very important to them. Dime just got moved into his new stall last week. Before that he lived next to Penny for—how long, Stevie?" asked Lisa. Stevie had ridden at Pine Hollow the longest.

Stevie shook her head, but she was starting to look excited. "I don't know," she said. "Years and years. Ever since I can remember."

"His being lonesome for her would explain everything," Lisa said. "He's not eating because he's sad. He's pinning his ears back and trying to bite us whenever we put him in his stall, because he wants to go back to his old stall. He's acting so atrocious in lessons—and at that games practice—because he gets so excited whenever he sees Penny again."

"Penny's been acting a little weird, too, come to think of it," Carole said. "Remember how bad she was at Cross County? She's not as upset as Dime, though. I don't know, Lisa. I think what you're saying makes sense, I just never would have

116

guessed that Dime had any special feelings for Penny."

"He's just a shaggy little lesson pony," Stevie said. "He doesn't seem like the romantic type."

"Oh, come on," Lisa protested. "Why should Dime's appearance have anything to do with his feelings?"

Carole grinned and grabbed her coat. "It shouldn't. After all, I wouldn't have guessed Mrs. Reg was the romantic type either, until I saw her react to what Mr. Stowe said. Poor Dime! I hope you're right, Lisa. We can cure him so easily."

"I know I'm right," Lisa replied.

Stevie grabbed her coat, too. "Let's go!"

LISA'S MOTHER DROVE past the hay barn and dropped them off at the main stable. A single light shone through a window of the hay barn, but the rest of Pine Hollow was dark and quiet; everyone had left to get ready for the party. Lisa flipped the stable's aisle lights on. Most of the horses were eating their dinners, and they looked up, still chewing contentedly, as The Saddle Club rushed past their stalls.

"I'll get Romeo," Stevie said. The gelding had been put in Dime's old stall, next to Penny. Stevie quickly put his halter on. "I'll get Romeo's dinner," Lisa offered. She grabbed his grain bucket and took it out into the aisle.

"Don't forget his water bucket," Stevie said. "Maybe I could hold him out here while you fix up the stall?" Romeo was already plunging his nose into his grain bucket, which Lisa had set on the aisle floor. "Romeo's not going anywhere until he's finished his oats."

"Good idea." Lisa grabbed a pitchfork and hastily tidied the stall. Red had already cleaned it thoroughly that afternoon, so she didn't have much to do.

Meanwhile, Carole had gone straight to Dime. She slid the stall door open, and the little pony pinned his ears back at her. His grain sat untouched in his bucket. "You poor darling," Carole crooned. At her sympathetic tone Dime relaxed slightly, and Carole gently slid his halter on. "Don't worry. We're taking you home."

She led him down the aisle. Dime lagged behind her, then suddenly seemed to notice where they were heading. His ears came forward. His eyes brightened. He began to walk with a jaunty swing to his step. By the time Carole got to Romeo, little Dime was almost trotting.

"Look at him!" Lisa exalted. Dime looked *happy*.

Penny thrust her head over her door and whinnied at Dime. Dime whinnied back, a long, high-pitched squeal. Romeo, bored now that his grain was gone, thrust his nose at Stevie to see if she had more.

"I'll get Dime's buckets!" Lisa rushed back to his stall. Stevie followed her more slowly, leading Romeo. Carole brought Dime to the door of his old stall. She unclipped the lead rope, and Dime rushed in. He sniffed all four corners. Carole gently shut the stall door. Dime came up to it and leaned over until his nose just touched Penny's. The ponies nickered to each other.

Lisa and Stevie came back carrying Dime's feed and water buckets. They stopped next to Carole. All three girls watched appreciatively as the two ponies nuzzled each other contentedly. Finally Dime turned away. He sniffed the grain in his bucket, then began to eat.

Carole found that tears had come to her eyes. "You poor pony," she whispered. "We're so sorry we took you away from your sweetheart."

119

"We won't do it again," Lisa promised.

"Do what again?" asked Max. The girls turned. Max had just come into the stable, and he was obviously dressed for the dance. He wore clean blue jeans, a red Shaker sweater over a red flannel shirt, and a pair of jazzy cowboy boots. His hair was still damp from a shower. "I saw the lights in the stable, and I wondered if something was wrong," he said.

"Something was wrong, but we fixed it," Lisa said. The Saddle Club explained how Carole's joke had made them realize what Dime's problem was.

"He and Penny are really attached to one another," Stevie said. "He just couldn't stand to be away from her." As Stevie said this, Dime left his grain bucket, stuck his head over his door, and touched noses briefly with Penny. Then he resumed eating.

"A pony kiss!" said Lisa.

Max shook his head, but he was smiling. "You girls are right; you must be," he said. "I can't believe I never thought of it myself. You know, lots of times when horses get really attached to one another, they act obnoxious about it—they want to be ridden side by side, or they have fits when

120

one is ridden and the other stays in the stable. Dime and Penny are so sweet all the time that I never recognized they were friends." He ruffled Dime's shaggy mane. "I'm sorry, buddy. We were only trying to give you a nicer stall. We won't do it again."

"Do you think he'll be entirely better now?" asked Carole. "We were so worried about him."

"We'll let Judy finish those blood tests to be sure," Max replied. "But I think we can safely assume that he'll be fine." He checked his watch. "Hey, it's time to start this dance, and lots of cars were pulling up when I ducked in here. You all don't want to miss the first dance, do you?"

Lisa grabbed Stevie's arm. "It's your song, remember?"

Stevie looked confused. "My song?"

" 'Just As Long As We're Together.' "

"Oh. Phil's and my song."

"That's right," Lisa said. "You don't want to miss it, do you?"

Stevie shook her head. "I don't want to miss him," she said.

"What?" asked Lisa.

"Nothing." Stevie found herself wondering whether she wouldn't rather be in some smelly cafeteria—with Phil—after all. Still, that would be against her principles—wouldn't it? *Look how happy Dime is*, she thought. *He could have had a nicer stall, but all he wanted was to stay close to Penny.*

"Stevie, are you coming?" asked Carole.

"Sure." She had made her choice. It was too late now.

THE SADDLE CLUB followed Max across the driveway. A dozen cars were parked outside the hay barn. Light spilled from all the windows and from the door whenever it opened to let another person inside. They could hear people talking and laughing.

Max opened the door. "Ohhh!" The Saddle Club gasped in unison. The barn was bathed in soft, rosy light. In the center, hanging from the main rafter, a glittering mirror ball slowly revolved. Rose-colored spotlights, nestled among the streamers in the corners, shone directly on the mirror ball, so that the entire barn shimmered with moving pink light.

"It's beautiful!" gasped Carole.

"It's Mr. Stowe's surprise," Stevie said, realizing that it must be. "Wow. He was right. This is the most romantic atmosphere I've ever seen." She swallowed hard. What good was atmosphere when you were alone?

Max tapped her on the shoulder to move her through the doorway. "Let's start the show," he said. He strode across the room and flicked the button on the stereo. "Ladies and gentlemen," he said, "Happy Valentine's Day!" He flicked another button, and the music began.

As soon as the first strains sounded, people began to choose partners, while others melted to the sides of the room. Lisa looked around avidly, wanting to see who was there. Adam led a blushing Betsy (Was she blushing, or had her mother let her wear makeup?) into the center of the floor. Several of the adult riders paired off, and May, Jasmine, Corey, and their old friend Joey Dutton started what looked like a game of ring-around-a-rosy. And there was Simon—Lisa caught her breath. He was so handsome! He had his arm around a black-haired girl whose back was to them. Lisa sighed. So Veronica had won after all.

"Excuse me," said a rude voice behind her. "You're blocking the door. I know you might not be planning on dancing tonight, Lisa, but I'd like to be able to get to the dance floor. So move."

Lisa gaped. It was Veronica! So who was the girl with Simon? On the dance floor Simon gently swung her around, and Lisa could see it was no one she recognized. Simon had probably brought someone from his own school.

"Look, Stevie," Lisa said, nudging her friend. "Veronica didn't get her hooks into him after all! The pink breeches weren't enough!"

"As if any color breeches would be enough to camouflage Veronica," Carole said. "Eew."

Stevie didn't say anything. Lisa glanced at her worriedly. Usually Stevie wouldn't miss a chance to insult Veronica.

"Are you okay?" she asked.

"Sure," Stevie said. On the stereo, the song hit its chorus: "Just as long, just as long, just as long as we're to-ge-e-e-ther . . ." Stevie sighed.

"Well, maybe we should get some chips— ohmigosh! Look!" Carole pointed across the crowd. "I never thought—I never guessed—oh, no!"

Lisa and Stevie looked where she pointed. Across the room, Mr. Stowe was leading a blushing Mrs. Reg onto the dance floor. He stopped for a moment, holding her hand, and then he pulled a small rose out of the pocket of his sports coat and gently pinned it to her lapel. Then he picked up her hands again and swung her into a slow dance.

"It's a romance," Lisa said, thunderstruck. "Right under our eyes. Like Dime and Penny— and we never even noticed!"

Mrs. Reg looked up at Mr. Stowe with sparkling eyes. Mr. Stowe smiled down at her happily. The signs were unmistakable.

"I knew it! I knew Mrs. Reg liked Mr. Stowe!" Carole exclaimed. "But I didn't know he liked her, too. This explains everything! He wasn't interested in riding nearly as much as he was interested in Mrs. Reg. He was riding so he could be around her."

"And he wasn't bothering her," Lisa said. "She liked it."

Carole clapped her hand over her mouth. "We spent so much time trying to keep him away from her! We could have wrecked everything!"

"We were awful," Stevie said with heartfelt vehemence. "We interfered with them every time they had a chance to be alone. Remember? We even made Mr. Stowe clean stalls instead of going on a trail ride with Mrs. Reg!"

"We meant well," Lisa said. She felt mortified.

"The problem is, they're like Dime and Penny. We never thought of them as being romantic, so we didn't see their friendship even when it was right in front of us."

They watched Mr. Stowe twirl Mrs. Reg around. They watched Mrs. Reg laugh.

"He's a good dancer," said Carole. "He's much more graceful than when he rides."

"He's not all that old, really," Lisa said. "He's not any older than Mrs. Reg. We're just used to thinking of Mrs. Reg as young, because she acts young."

"Mr. Stowe acts young, too," Stevie said, thinking of the glitter ball and all the work he had so cheerfully done around the stable. "Think about it. We might have broken them up before they had a chance to get together!" She couldn't believe she'd been so blind.

"At least we didn't," Carole said. "That's one Saddle Club project that I'm glad failed."

Stevie bit her lip. She longed to be out on the dance floor—with Phil. She wanted to feel as happy as Mrs. Reg looked. More than anything else, she realized, she wanted to be with Phil.

"I made a big mistake," she said slowly. "I shouldn't have insisted that Phil come here. He probably shouldn't have insisted I go to his dance, either, but at least I've figured it out now. The important thing isn't which dance we go to. More than anything else, I wish I were with him right now."

Carole and Lisa looked at her sympathetically. "We thought you might feel like that in the end," Lisa said.

"It's not that I don't want to be with you guys—"

"Of course not," Carole said. "We know we're your best friends."

"I think I still can be with Phil," Stevie said determinedly. "I'm going to go use Mrs. Reg's phone. This is an emergency if I ever saw one."

Carole and Lisa smiled. Mrs. Reg's phone was strictly off-limits, except for emergencies.

"I'm going to call my mom and ask her to come get me," Stevie continued. "I'm going to Phil's dance."

12

Mr. Stowe came up to Lisa and made a deep bow. "May I have the honor of a waltz?" he asked in a courtly tone.

Lisa giggled. Even without Stevie, she and Carole were having a marvelous time. They had danced to some of the faster tunes, and during the slow dances they had had the fun of watching Simon twirl his date around the floor while Veronica glared from the sidelines in fury.

"I'd love to dance the way you do," Lisa said, "but I don't know how." She'd been admiring Mr. Stowe's elegance for half an hour. He and Mrs. Reg both danced very well.

Mr. Stowe held out his hand. "If you don't know the waltz, I'll teach you," he said. He led her to an open space on the floor, then showed her how to place her hands. "Up on your toes," he commanded. Lisa, surprised, lifted her heels off the floor. She hadn't thought waltzing would be like ballet. "Now, follow my lead," he said. "*One*-two-three, *one*-two-three." Mr. Stowe counted to the music, and he and Lisa spun across the floor. Lisa hadn't known waltzing could be so much fun. She felt as if she had wings.

"Thank you," she said when the dance was over. She bit her lip. "Mr. Stowe—my friends and I didn't realize that you and Mrs. Reg—I mean—I mean, we're sorry we made you work so much."

Mr. Stowe smiled. "I always liked to work," he said. "I still do. But I guess Elizabeth kind of got the impression I was *only* interested in working. I talked to her and we've got that straightened out now, so don't worry about it."

Lisa was very glad The Saddle Club hadn't messed things up permanently. "Thank you for showing me the waltz."

"You're welcome," he replied. "Now I'll take Carole for a spin, if she'd like. Where's Stevie?"

"She left a little bit ago. She had another dance to go to." Lisa got herself a drink and watched Mr. Stowe sweep Carole around the floor. From the look on Carole's face, she was enjoying it just as much as Lisa had.

Lisa put down her drink. "Hey, Max," she said. "Want to waltz?"

Max had spent most of the evening with his wife, Deborah, but had only danced once so far. At Lisa's suggestion Deborah laughed, and Max looked a little sheepish. "I managed to duck dance classes when I was young," he said. "I don't know how to waltz."

"That's okay," Lisa said. "I'll teach you."

Max laughingly agreed, but Lisa discovered that it was much harder to waltz when neither person knew what he or she was doing. "You're supposed to lead me around," she instructed. "*One*-two-three, *one*-two-three. Like that." She pointed at Mr. Stowe and Carole.

Max shook his head. "I can't do that. You lead."

"Okay." Lisa took a deep breath. "Get up on your toes."

"No way," said Max.

"Okay, just walk normally. Ready?" She tried to steer Max. First she stepped on his foot, then he stepped on hers, then they both tripped.

Max grinned and dropped his hands. "Why don't I buy you a drink?" he joked. He walked with her over to the hay-bale table where free drinks had been set out for everyone. In a moment the dance ended, and Carole joined them.

"Phew, that was fun!" she said. To Max she added, "I saw you out there with Lisa. Maybe you should get Mr. Stowe to show you how to do it."

Max roared with laughter. "No, I think I'll just watch from now on," he said. He went to rejoin Deborah, but Deborah shook her head at him and waltzed with Mr. Stowe. Mrs. Reg adjusted the volume on the stereo, then walked out to the dance floor and cut in on Deborah. Deborah laughed, patted Mrs. Reg on the shoulder, and walked back to Max.

Carole and Lisa sat down on a hay bale. "Do you think it's true love?" Lisa asked, nodding toward Mrs. Reg.

"Too soon to tell," Carole said. "But it's a happy Valentine's Day."

A skinny boy who looked a few years younger

than the girls sat down on the hay bale next to
Lisa. "Hi," he said nervously. He took a few sips
of his drink.

Lisa looked at Carole, who shook her head.
Neither of them recognized him.

"Hi," Carole said. "I'm Carole and this is Lisa.
Are you one of the Cross County riders?"

The boy nodded enthusiastically. "I'm Dusty,"
he said. "I remember you, Lisa." He looked at her
adoringly. "You fell off twice last weekend at our
games."

Lisa felt a blush creep up her neck. "How nice
of you to remember," she told him.

"Thanks." The boy nodded and scooted a little
closer to her. "I saw you dancing. Would you
show me how to waltz?"

Lisa didn't know what to say that wouldn't
hurt his feelings. She didn't want to dance with
him.

Carole suddenly coughed, then choked. "Choking—on a—chip!" she wheezed. She hacked a
few more times, grabbed Lisa's hand, and gasped,
"Lisa—help!" They raced to the other side of the
room and disappeared behind a stack of hay bales
near the door.

"I'd try the Heimlich maneuver," Lisa said,

rolling with silent laughter, "except that you can't be choking. You weren't eating any chips!"

Carole grinned. "Maybe I was choking on my diet soda?" she suggested.

"Maybe," Lisa said. "Anyway, I'm glad you're all right now. And thanks. Are we going to have to dodge Dusty for the rest of the evening?"

"I don't think we both are," Carole said. "Just you."

Lisa rolled her eyes. "I'm the one that stands out, after all—you didn't fall off!"

"No," Carole said. "Penny was running away with me so fast last weekend that Dusty probably never got to see my face at all."

"Trade you," offered Lisa. "I'll take the runaway, you can have the falls and Dusty."

"Nope," said Carole. "But I'm willing to choke on imaginary potato chips all night long, whenever you need me."

A flash of headlights shone through the windows, and they heard a car come to an abrupt stop on the gravel drive. A few seconds later someone threw open the door.

"Phil!" Lisa said, scrambling to her feet. She and Carole ran to meet him. "What are you doing here? Where's Stevie?"

Phil looked startled, as well as out of breath. "Dancing?" he guessed. "Sitting on a hay bale? Talking to you guys? I don't know! You tell me."

"She's at your school," Carole said. "She came here and decided she missed you too much, so she left for your dance."

Phil groaned. He staggered over to a hay bale, sat down, and covered his face with his hands. When he uncovered it he was laughing. "I went to my dance," he said. "And when I got there I saw all these couples dancing, and I thought, *This is really stupid*. More than anything else, I just wanted to be with Stevie. So I called my mom and had her drive me over here."

"That's really ironic," said Lisa. "When you think about it—"

"—it's really nice," Carole interrupted. "You both did the right thing."

"Yeah, but . . ." Phil shook his head. "Stevie doesn't know very many people from my school, and my dance was really crowded. She's not going to know where I am!"

Carole looked at Lisa. "Definitely," Lisa said in response to Carole's unspoken question. "This definitely counts as an emergency."

"Come on," Carole said, pulling Phil to his feet. "Mrs. Reg has a phone in her office."

When they reached the office, they found to their surprise that the phone was already ringing. Lisa grabbed it. "Good evening, Pine Hollow Stables," she said politely. She was greeted with hysterical laughter—laughter she knew very well.

"Phil, it's Stevie," Lisa said, holding the phone out to him. "I think she's figured out where you are."

IN THE CROWDED, noisy hallway of Phil's school, Stevie pressed the phone closer to her ear. "Happy Valentine's Day!" she shouted.

"Happy Valentine's Day to you, too!" Phil shouted back.

"I'm sorry," she said.

"So am I!" he replied. "And I'm sorry we're not at the same dance, too. Have you found anyone you know?"

"Oh, sure," Stevie said cheerfully. "I saw A.J. and Bart as soon as I walked in—that's how I knew where you were. They're right here." She waved her fingers at Phil's two closest friends. They were in Cross County, so she'd hung around them a lot at Pony Club events.

"I hate to say this, Stevie," Phil continued, "but my mom is absolutely going to die if I ask her to come get me again."

"Mine too," Stevie said. "Are you having an awful time?"

"No. I can hang around Carole and Lisa, if they don't mind."

Lisa grabbed the phone. "Of course we don't mind," she said, just as a male voice on the other end said, "We'll take care of her, Phil."

"Hi, A.J.!" Lisa said.

"Hi, Lisa!" he answered.

Stevie grabbed the phone back. "Hi, Lisa! Put Phil back on, please. Hi, Phil. Hey, next time I'll plan to go to your dance from the start, okay?"

"No, I'll plan to go to *yours*," Phil said.

Stevie laughed. "Whatever. Let's just both plan to go to the same one."

"Okay."

They talked a bit more and then Stevie hung up the phone. It was a good Valentine's Day after all.

Carole and Lisa had stepped outside the office to give Phil a few moments to talk to Stevie alone. When he rejoined them, they grinned at each other.

"Do you guys have any food here?" he asked. "I was too busy hanging streamers—and being upset about Stevie—to eat any dinner."

"We've got chips," Lisa said.

"Real and imaginary," Carole added, and both girls broke out laughing. Phil looked mystified.

"Never mind," Carole said. "What can you tell us about a kid in your Pony Club named Dusty?"

Phil laughed. "Dusty? Is he here? First of all, he's only in the sixth grade. And Dusty's not his real name. We call him Dusty because he falls off his horse so often the seat of his breeches is always dusty."

Lisa and Carole howled. "That explains his attraction to Lisa," Carole said when she could speak.

"Phil," Lisa said with a shake of her head, "why couldn't you have brought a friend? It would make dodging Dusty so much easier!"

13

CAROLE LOOKED OUT the window of Lisa's bedroom. "Here's Stevie now," she announced.

"Oh, good." Lisa joined Carole at the window. They watched Stevie get out of her mother's car and run up the steps to Lisa's house, and they watched Mrs. Lake drive away.

Carole and Lisa had come home from Pine Hollow first, half an hour before. They'd changed into comfy sweatpants and shirts, then stockpiled snacks in Lisa's room. Of course, they couldn't really discuss the whole night until Stevie arrived.

Stevie burst through the door. "I'm back!" she cried. "How was your dance? Did you have fun?"

She tossed her coat on the floor and pulled off her boots.

"We really did," Carole replied. "Phil is always fun to hang around, and Mr. Stowe waltzed with both of us twice—"

"Mr. Stowe?" asked Stevie. "Why wasn't he dancing with Mrs. Reg?"

"Oh, he was, it's just—"

"Go change your clothes and come sit down," Lisa said. "Then we can talk about everything in order."

"Yes, ma'am!" Stevie grinned and saluted. "What this Saddle Club needs is organization!"

Lisa threw a pretzel at her. Stevie ducked and ran into the bathroom. Lisa grinned. A long, long time ago, when they had first started The Saddle Club, Lisa had tried to make up a lot of rules. They didn't work out well. The two that lasted were the only important ones, Lisa thought— being horse-crazy, and helping each other. She smiled. Between Stevie and Dime, she felt as if she'd done both today. Then she laughed.

"What are you thinking about?" Carole asked, looking at her strangely.

"You—keeping me away from Dusty!"

Carole snorted and joined in her laughter. When Stevie came back into the room, Lisa said in an orderly voice, "Stephanie, now you can tell us about your dance."

Stevie plopped down on one of Lisa's cushions. "You know, I had a really great time," she said. "It was weird, because aside from A.J. and Bart I only saw two other people whose names I even knew. But A.J. and Bart introduced me to some of their friends, and everyone was nice. Plus, I didn't have to feel self-conscious about how I looked when I was dancing. None of those people are ever going to see me again!"

"Unless you go to Phil's dance next year," Lisa teased.

Stevie looked thoughtful. "True. Well, in that case, maybe I'll wear a wig."

She smiled and continued. "I have to admit, Phil really did do a great job on his decorations. The place didn't look or smell like a cafeteria at all!" She tossed the sweater she'd borrowed back to Carole. "Smell," she directed.

Carole sniffed. "You're right, it doesn't smell like a cafeteria. It doesn't smell like anything."

"That's a good thing, isn't it?" asked Lisa.

Carole laughed. "*I* think so."

Stevie opened some of the cans of soda Lisa had brought up and passed them around. Lisa poured the pretzels into a bowl so that they could all eat at once. "So, you had a good Valentine's after all," she said to Stevie.

Stevie lay back and looked thoughtfully at the ceiling. "In a way, I had the best day possible," she said. "I mean, I would rather have been with Phil, of course—but that's the point, isn't it? I figured out that being with Phil was what was important to me."

"And he figured out that being with you was what was important to him," Carole replied.

Stevie grinned. "Yeah. Wonderful, isn't it? It wasn't exactly the night of romance I was hoping for, but in some ways it's better. But tell me, what happened at Pine Hollow?"

"First of all, Dime really does seem better," Carole said excitedly.

Stevie sat up. "Well, sure. We expected that."

"No, we hoped it," Carole corrected her. "That's not quite the same thing."

"Anyway," Lisa said, "we went back to check on him when the dance was over. He was sound asleep, lying down—but he was lying with his back right against the wall next to Penny's stall!"

"And on the other side," Carole said, "Penny was sleeping with her back right against the wall next to Dime!"

"It was the sweetest thing I ever saw," Lisa said. "I never would have guessed he was so attached to her. We didn't wake him, but we're sure he's going to be fine."

"Thanks to Lisa, who figured it out," Carole said. Lisa grinned. She did feel just a little proud of herself. "Dime ate all his grain, too," Carole reported.

"Great," Stevie said. "Now, tell me about this waltzing stuff. Why wasn't Mr. Stowe dancing with Mrs. Reg?"

"Oh, he was. He danced at least half the dances with her! I think he was just dancing with us to be nice." Lisa smiled, remembering her airy waltzes. "He's a very good dancer."

"We didn't dance with anybody else," reported Carole. "We were a little busy—avoiding a new admirer of Lisa's."

Stevie shrieked and demanded to know all the details. Lisa and Carole told her the whole story of Dusty. "In the end, you'll never guess who danced with him!" said Carole. "Veronica!"

Stevie's mouth fell open. "No!"

"Seriously. I don't know why—except she was getting pretty desperate, I think. Simon wasn't even noticing her. The girl he brought to the dance seemed really nice. And I guess Dusty was wearing some kind of designer clothes—we didn't really notice until he took the dance floor, but you know how that kind of thing appeals to Veronica. He seemed like an okay guy, you know, except that he was so young—"

"—and that he only liked me because he thought I was a bad rider!" Lisa cut in.

"He might have had other reasons," Carole said supportively.

"Who cares?" Lisa asked. "One thing I learned tonight was that I don't need a boyfriend to have a nice time at a dance."

"Me either," said Carole emphatically.

"Me either!" Stevie said with a laugh.

"Mrs. Reg, on the other hand . . ." Lisa giggled. "If I didn't know better, I'd swear she was flirting!"

"She *was* flirting!" Carole said. "And Mr. Stowe was flirting back!" She turned to Stevie. "That's one thing I'm sorry you missed. I was really glad that all our interference didn't stop them from—well—from flirting. From getting to know each other."

"I can't believe we didn't realize what was going on." Stevie groaned, but the groan turned into a yawn. "I hate to say this, but I'm beat. Rock, paper, scissors for the bed."

"One, two, three!" Stevie and Carole both threw scissors. Lisa threw rock, so she won.

"Ha," she said, climbing into her own bed.

"It's only fair," Stevie said. She and Carole rolled out their sleeping bags. Stevie moved the snacks to the top of Lisa's dresser, where she could find them if she happened to be hungry in the night.

"Mr. Stowe might not be the best rider in the world," Carole said as she climbed into her sleeping bag, "but he's an awfully nice person. Mrs. Reg deserves someone as nice as him. And he probably likes horses enough. I can't imagine Mrs. Reg getting serious about anyone who didn't ride at all."

"Deborah hardly rode before she met Max," Lisa reminded them.

"Yeah," said Stevie, settling onto her pillow with a sigh. "As long as Mr. Stowe has the riding ability to handle nice, long, romantic trail rides, that's probably all he needs. And he does, so it'll be okay."

A sudden thought made Lisa giggle. "I forgot to tell even you, Carole," she said. "While you were dancing your second waltz with Mr. Stowe, Mrs. Reg came up to me and accused me of making her seem like an old witch! She said that somehow poor Howard—that's what she called Mr. Stowe, poor Howard—got the impression that he had to work around the stable all the time in order to impress her!"

Stevie and Carole laughed appreciatively. "What did you say?" asked Carole.

"I told her that *we* had to work all the time in order to impress her," Lisa said. "She just drew herself up and said, kind of royally, 'There's a time for work and a time for play!'" Lisa yawned and reached for the light switch.

"I guess Mrs. Reg has found her time for play," Stevie said.

"I'm happy for her—and for Mr. Stowe, and Dime, and you, Stevie," said Lisa. She turned out the light.

"Oh," Carole said as the room was plunged into darkness, "but don't you wish there were a few decent boys at Pine Hollow!"

ABOUT THE AUTHOR

BONNIE BRYANT is the author of many books for young readers, including novelizations of movie hits such as *Teenage Mutant Ninja Turtles* and *Honey, I Blew Up the Kid*, written under her married name, B. B. Hiller.

Ms. Bryant began writing The Saddle Club in 1986. Although she had done some riding before that, she intensified her studies then and found herself learning right along with her characters Stevie, Carole, and Lisa. She claims that they are all much better riders than she is.

Ms. Bryant was born and raised in New York City. She still lives there, in Greenwich Village, with her two sons.

Don't miss Bonnie Bryant's next exciting Saddle Club adventure . . .

Horse Capades
The Saddle Club #64

Practical joker Stevie has decided to reform. The only problem is, nobody believes her. Things get worse for poor Stevie when she tries to shoot a movie for school—*Cinderella on Horseback*. After all, just because she's given up playing pranks on people doesn't mean she's given up wild schemes. No one in the cast cooperates because they're sure Stevie is trying to set them up to look like fools. That's when Stevie decides she has to revert to her old practical-joking ways . . . and then some. Watch out, Pine Hollow!

Saddle Up For Fun!
Join The
Saddle Club

As an official Saddle Club member you'll get:

- *Saddle Club newsletter*
- *Saddle Club membership card*
- *Saddle Club bookmark*
- *and exciting updates on everything that's happening with your favorite series.*

Bantam Doubleday Dell Books for Young Readers
Saddle Club Membership Box BK
1540 Broadway
New York, NY 10036

SKYLARK

Bantam Doubleday Dell
Books for Young Readers

Name _____

Address _____

City _____ State _____ Zip _____

Date of birth _____

Offer good while supplies last.

BFYR - 8/93